PROOF OF PURPLE

proof of purple

J.C. Buchanan

Amethyst Publishing

Published by Amethyst Publishing

Text Copyright ©2018 by J.C. Buchanan

ISBN 9780692170205

www.jcbuchanan.com

Typeset in Adobe Garamond Pro.

Printed in the United States of America.

Do not be overcome by evil,
but overcome evil with good.

Romans 12:21

Reading the memorial poem at my best friend's departure proved to be the hardest thing I had ever done in my life, far surpassing all the fears my imagination had festered upon in those troubling weeks leading up to this moment.

Those dark times when I hardly slept, staying up late into the night, unable to rid myself of the creepy feeling up and down my spine, and the images that flashed through my mind like an illness, creating the nauseating feeling in my stomach and the swimmy, sick feeling in my head that made sleep—or even rest—impossible. Those dark times when I made my way through the day like wading through thick and impassable waters, dark and deep and brooding and rising more as I walked through them, swallowing me and suffocating me, stealing my very breath the more I tried to walk. Those dark times when tears seemed endless and sorrow seemed eternal.

My best friend was alive, but she was leaving.

Forever.

As far as I was concerned, she was dead. After to-night, after this departure, she might as well be. I'd release her, release the memories, in the form of a sweet memorial—a poem I now held in my hand. I would acknowledge she was wrong to those around me. Let her go. And then life would move on again, like she never existed.

They told me it was normal to feel rebellious against society in moments like these, but to be careful to not let it get to me. I tried my best to listen to them. It was just so tough.

Swallowing hard, I stared down at the paper with its bold, black words glaring up at me, trying to prepare myself for the moment when I'd step out into the spotlight, in front of the crowd of people who soon would deny the existence of the girl sitting left stage with her face buried in her arms. In front of them I'd say—boldly and confidently—that I knew she was a disgrace and I was letting her go. I'd read the farewell poem I composed for her. It all seemed so regulatory, so simple. I tried to focus only on that: the routine. Routine could get me through. Standards could get me through. This world, perfectly designed and strategized, could get me through.

But mere thoughts could only sustain my outward appearance. I stepped up, the crumpled paper within my sweaty grasp, and risked a glance at my broken friend, right as she raised her face for the first time that evening to meet my eyes. Our gaze held for a long moment when it seemed like seconds became hours and silent communication flashed between us in the form of images and memories, both good and bad, reminding me of all that we had and all that had happened. No amount of standard or reminder of society could hold me together on the inside, and I fought to make sense of this reality—this reality that they were taking my best friend away from me, forever, and I could do nothing except read a sentimental poem letting the world know I was letting her go along with all the turmoil and confusion she'd brought.

Nobody got withdrawn in high school.

Until my best friend did.

I cleared my throat, my eyes scanning around, searching, longing for somewhere to rest, until I found myself staring into one of the bright lights. Anything to distract my mind from the fact that she was staring at me.

I trembled and forced my gaze down to the paper in my hands: this paper honoring her life and releasing her peacefully from my own. Letting her go, in order to prevent chaos and frustration among us. It was my duty as one of those closest to her to set an example. I'd grown up with this standard. Knew it as well as I knew anything else about my world. Never did I expect to actually have to follow through with the regulation myself.

My eyes wouldn't obey me, and instinctively I was

looking at my friend again. Her wobbly gaze pierced me. Twisted me. Whispers in my ear told me in a few weeks this would all be past me. I only had to get through these next few moments and life could go on. Life could move on beyond this. For the best.

But everything else in me screamed against those words holding me prisoner and I tried to speak, wondering how long I had been standing there, but finding words yet impossible. Every fiber of me strained to break loose, scream, and squeeze my friend as if my arms could have any power against the world around me.

And suddenly, as equal as the force pulling me towards her were the eyes of the community and my world following my every move: the kind faces encouraging me that I could do this, reminding me that it was only a few sentences, promising me it'd all be alright. And I felt myself carefully reconstructing the barrier around the cavern of sadness that had been pooling within my heart, swallowing my grief, and focusing only on what my world had told me, this world that hadn't yet failed me.

Someone said my name, and for a split second I heard my best friend's voice, but it was only the director, kindly reminding me I had a duty to perform. "Are you going to go?"

I did, swallowing back my sadness and shoving away the turmoil, focusing only on the words, reading them robotically in hope they could become genuine but knowing they never would without my emotion also becoming transparent. With a clear voice I presented my tribute to my friend's life and how I was ready to let go and move on. When I finished, I opened my hands, letting the paper flutter to the floor where it fell into the folds of the other papers of those who had presented before me, and then I turned to leave to find a spot in the goodbye line. As I turned, I caught her eye again, and the look in her eyes this time would stay with me for what would seem like centuries—a look that didn't ask *why*, as so many withdrawees begged their family members, or even a look that communicated anger or disdain. Either of those I could have taken. Instead, it was the desperation on her face, the ultimate hopelessness that begged *help me*, that haunted my dreams at night.

That night my best friend was withdrawn from our world—not dead, but never to be seen again: this girl to whom I'd pledged absolute loyalty pleaded with me to fulfill all my now-empty promises to always be there for her and help her when she called. But instead of replying, I turned and walked away.

risa | PART 1

7:10 Rise

Get out of bed/extra time	(2 min)
Get dressed	(3 min)
Make bed	(5 min)
Brush teeth & wash face	(4 min)
Hairstyle	(5 min)
Shoes on	(1 min)

7:30 Breakfast
7:45 Leave home
7:50 Bus
7:55 Arrive at school
8:10 School Commences
8:10 English
9:20 Math
10:30 Science
11:40 History
12:45 Lunch & Recess
1:45 Extracurricular
2:45 Extracurricular
2:45 School Ends
2:55 Board Bus
3:00 Arrive Home
3:05 Rest Period
4:00 Social
5:45 Dinner Preparations
6:00 Dinner
6:30 Cleanup
6:45 Study
7:30 Family Time
8:00 Relax Period
8:40 Shower
9:00 Prepare for Bed

Pajamas on	(3 min)
Brush teeth/wash face	(4 min)
Clean room	(7 min)
Hairstyle	(5 min)

9:30 Quiet Time
10:00 Lights Out

8

Two months, one week, and three days since Risa had last seen her best friend.

And there was nobody she could talk to about it.

She and Mirren weren't best friends anymore.

And to this world, Mirren had never even existed.

After Mirren left, her family had to decide what to do with her belongings; nonexistent people didn't own things. They threw most of it away, as was custom, but they also chose to do what many commonly did and disperse Mirren's more personal belongings to those who had been close to her. One month after Mirren left, her older sister, Emory, showed up at Risa's door, her face gray and expressionless and a cardboard box in her arms. "My family wants you to have this," she said, shoving the box at Risa. It had barely landed in Risa's arms before Emory was already turning to leave.

Had Emory's sister been anyone other than Mirren, had Mirren just been "Emory's sister," Risa might have called out after her with her condolences, maybe some words of comfort. But Mirren wasn't just "Emory's sister."

She was Risa's best friend.

If they even could be called that anymore—best friends. But now that there would never be any way to work things out, it was just easier to remember the good memories and pretend it had still been the reality when she left.

Time went by, and nothing changed. So she bit down on her lip and went about her days, trying to maintain the act that she was fine, *fine,* fine—of course she was fine.

Her best friend was gone. Never to return. She had been taken from them and Risa had done nothing to stop it. Somewhere she was out there, still alive and breathing, but Risa would never see her again.

The practices and habits she began to develop were nowhere near standard behavior, but surely this was the exception to the usual two-week grieving period: this situation was so unusual, so rare, so unexpected—that she would experience so much in just one summer—that of course it would take her longer to get past this. Because there wasn't just grief, but also the betrayal. The betrayal that sometimes she didn't even fully believe all that had happened.

Children often got withdrawn. That was one thing.

But nobody got withdrawn in high school.

She expected her parents to be on her case about the

schedule she wasn't following and the standards she was letting slide. But they didn't even so much as comment on it, and she wasn't sure how she felt about that. Of course she wanted to feel better. It was when that picture of feeling better had to correlate with forgetting people she'd loved that it became so difficult.

She hated this. She hated her new reality. Her life. She hated her world. And she hated all the hating she was doing. But she had no idea how to change it.

saige | PART 2

SPRING SCHEDULES - HIGH SCHOOL LEVEL STUDENT #287 -
SAIGE RAENA PEMBERTON

7:10 Rise

Get out of bed/extra time	(2 min)
Get dressed	(3 min)
Make bed	(5 min)
Brush teeth & wash face	(4 min)
Hairstyle	(5 min)
Shoes on	(1 min)

7:30 Breakfast

7:45 Leave home

7:50 Bus

7:55 Arrive at school

8:10 School Commences

8:10 Math

9:20 Science

10:30 English

11:40 History

12:45 Lunch & Recess

1:45 Extracurricular

2:45 Extracurricular

2:45 School Ends

2:55 Board Bus

3:00 Arrive Home

3:05 Rest Period

4:00 Social

5:45 Dinner Preparations

6:00 Dinner

6:30 Cleanup

6:45 Study

7:30 Family Time

8:00 Relax Period

8:40 Shower

9:00 Prepare for Bed

Pajamas on	(3 min)
Brush teeth/wash face	(4 min)
Clean room	(7 min)
Hairstyle	(5 min)

9:30 Quiet Time

10:00 Lights Out

When Saige Pemberton arrived at the skating rink, there was no one waiting for her.

Absently she tugged her sweater tighter around her shoulders and checked the time on her watch, right as it beeped to signal the beginning of social hour. But there was still no sign of Brightly.

Awkwardly Saige stood on the sidewalk, in the middle of the bustling and jostling of people laughing with friends and others still maybe hurrying to meet friends. Buses honked, people laughed, shouted, and talked. Bells on shop doors rung and rung as people went in and out. Tires screeched. Watches beeped.

It was the world Saige had always known. The world she trusted, the world she knew and loved, full of people she knew and loved and who loved her.

But right now, all she could feel was loneliness. And

frustration. Not at Brightly, but with herself. Because this wasn't the first time she'd been stood up by her so-called friend, and somehow she was naive enough to still believe Brightly time and time again.

She should have thought ahead, had a plan in the back of her mind for something else to do during social hour when this happened. But she hadn't, and now she had to go home and turn in another daily schedule with a blank spot after the line for social. It wasn't the first blank schedule she'd turned in, and her parents would be furious. Archer would be so disappointed in her.

She grunted to herself and turned to trudge back up the streets, to at least look like she had somewhere to go, someone to see, something to do. Even though she had nothing.

Why hadn't she thought ahead of time? That Brightly could ditch her didn't come as a shocker, and she inwardly griped at herself for being so dumb as to miss this. But the truth was she hadn't missed it—she had just chosen not to see it. Because having a plan ready would have been admitting Brightly wasn't a true friend.

When she first met Brightly, almost a year ago now, she hadn't seen any of this—any of the signs that Brightly might not be a good person to be friends with. If she had, she wouldn't have befriended the chattery, clever girl with an eye for trouble and chaos. She had seen a bubbly girl with an obnoxious laugh and a witty personality, and so she had sat down right at her table during lunch one day and introduced herself.

She had been so bold back then. In the year since, a year full of odd remarks on Brightly's part, pointless conversations, and many, many days of leaving Saige behind to chase boys, Saige had found herself growing more and more reserved. Less and less like the Saige she had once been. Whether or not she liked who she was becoming was still something that was up in the air.

But of course, back then she had had the emotional drive she didn't have now. Destroying the relationship with her best friend did that to a person—gave them that emotional drive to prove that person wrong, to prove they didn't need that person, to prove that they were okay. That hadn't been Saige's motivation, though. She had been done with Linley for a long time before the friendship actually ended.

Now, she found herself at the end of the city block; ahead of her was Center Street, and beyond that, the rows of streets on which sat all the townhomes in which the citizens of the town lived. To her right was more downtown streets,

streets packed with stores and entertainment, and to her left was the park, and far beyond that, the factories that produced everything they needed, from food to clothing to home furnishings. She never really stopped to look at it; she was always caught up with friends or family.

How she wished these things didn't faze her—she wished she could somehow resurrect the bold part of her personality and find some new people to befriend. But now the idea seemed too intimidating; and she had been so closed off within her own friend group that she had no one else to turn to.

Though, she reminded herself, this didn't mean her friendship with Brightly was over. Brightly often got swept up in things and simply forgot; she had always known this about Brightly. That her friend could have just forgotten about her today comforted her from the standpoint that tomorrow she might still have someone for social.

Surely she could rule off today as just a mometary failure on Brightly's part. After all, no one was perfect, and tomorrow they could be back like nothing had ever happened.

"And so, after our Founders obtained control of this portion of land that we know and love as our home country and divided it into the subsequent communities, they set in place the standards of life—the standards that help define the qualities of our life and prevent problems that could hinder it. Standards that have since eliminated crimes, disease, conflict, and all other negative aspects of life. Thanks to their hard work at scheduling and standardizing, we now live in a world of peace, integrity, and intelligence. And you are the next generation. Upon your shoulders rests the important duty of upholding these standards, no matter the cost. Will you choose to rise to the occasion?"

Inwardly Saige sighed, propping her chin in her hands as she sat at her desk, trying to act like she was intently listening like the good student she was. But she already knew all of this, and had endured Mrs. Purcell's call-to-action lectures one too many times already this year. Her mind drifted, and she was thinking of Brightly again. Brightly, who hadn't talked to her at all today, even though they had passed each other twice in the halls between classes. Saige hated that it bothered her so much. So much for a peaceful world. She regretted the thought as soon as it passed through her mind. This was a peaceful world. They didn't deal with crime or war, and probably never would, and it was something she was truly thankful for. But standards could only dictate so much, and conflict between friends and family occurred more than the community preferred to admit.

"And now that we've concluded that review…it's the first of March, students. You know what that means." Mrs. Purcell shuffled through her binder of notes as the class bit back muted groans. Saige slumped lower in her seat as her teacher stood up abruptly, challenging each one of them with her gaze. "Test. Preparation."

A low sigh escaped Saige's lips. Spring was most definitely upon them.

"—I will be handing out updated Test booklets for this year at the end of class, so don't leave this room without one. Be sure to look through them carefully for the updated notes and information, as always." Mrs. Purcell began to pace. "Let's review the history of the Test and its importance. Ever since the Test was instituted—"

"Seventy-five years ago," one student volunteered,

and Mrs. Purcell stopped midstride to eye her. "That is correct, Katelyn, but you just interrupted me. You'd do well to watch your words. That's not a good habit to be in before Testing."

"Of course, Mrs. Purcell."

Saige twirled a pencil in her hand, watching the arc in made in the air, thinking of how Mrs. Purcell hadn't bothered to remind them that interrupting was against speaking standards. Perhaps she was loosening up regarding the lighter standards now that so much else was at stake.

"As I was saying. Ever since the Test was instituted seventy-five years ago, it has proven to be a flawless way to keep our society running the way it was intended to. To produce a society that is smart, aware, wise—a society that can truly uphold these standards. Students who score Purple—the highest scores. What are some qualities that are often present in such students? Annalise?"

"Honesty, compassion, kindness."

"That is correct. Additionally, Purple students are also some of the most brilliant minds of our society. Purple students—especially High Purples—are the students that will pave the way to not only upholding society, but improving it to make it the best it can be. Purple students are the ones we should be looking to to set the example when it comes to loyalty and integrity that the rest of us should be constantly striving toward.

"Now, I don't say this to dishonor any of you who may be Blue or Green or even Yellow students. There is no shame in being a student who is still growing. I believe you all have the capacity to be Purple, and I want you to know and believe you can get there.

"And now then: the students who score Red—the lowest scorers. Who are they? Yes, Risa?"

"Students who don't understand society?"

"Yes, but I'm looking for something more specific. Never mind, I'll just remind you myself. Red students are the students who either don't have the work ethic to score higher, or who simply don't have the mental ability to. Risa, tell me, are either of these persons helpful or contributable to our flawless society?"

"No, Mrs. Purcell."

"Correct. Well, then, what is to be done with students who score so low? Mirren?"

Saige looked over at the small-framed girl, her blonde braid pulled over one shoulder, her eyes lowering as she answered the dark question. "They are withdrawn from society, Mrs. Purcell."

Chills shot up Saige's spine like they always did at the mention of the word. She clenched her fists beneath her desk, trying to distract her mind.

"Elaborate," her teacher prompted.

Unclenching her fists, Saige carefully brought her

hands back up to rest on her desk, taking breaths in slowly, and before long felt the instinctual panic slip away, her tense muscles relax again.

Mirren cleared her throat, her gaze steady on the teacher as she sat up higher in her seat. "Students who score Red are considered harmful to our community and so are withdrawn from our community to prevent the spread of something dangerous or something that could hurt us in any way." She swallowed and took a breath before continuing, closing her eyes for a brief second.

This topic also made her uneasy, Saige realized, recognizing the symptoms of trying to keep one's anxiety in check.

"Red students who are withdrawn are taken away permanently, to avoid influencing others. To keep everything in check." She paused again, taking another breath. "To maintain this balance, Red students from all communities are sent to the Holding. A secure, contained area, outside country borders, where they will live the rest of their lives."

"Correct. Great answer, Mirren. Do you think this is a good standard?" She addressed the whole class now, and when no one volunteered, she said, "Saige, what do you think?"

Saige jumped a bit and, blinking quickly, got herself together best she could. "I think it's a smart and beneficial way to handle a harmful situation," she recited choppily, hoping her stutter didn't make an appearance. Being the only correct answer, her reply sent a smile across her teacher's face. "Excellent. I'm so glad we can all agree."

But as class continued, all that tossed through Saige's mind was how maybe she didn't completely agree.

When school ended, she left silently, not bothering to stop to talk to anyone and was so focused on just getting to the bus to get home that she didn't see Brightly until she was right in front of her.

"Look who it is. Saige Raena Pemberton!"

Saige crossed her arms. She was in no mood for this. "Where were you yesterday, Brightly?" Or maybe being so straightforward wasn't a good idea. Brightly's face twisted into an arrogant, offended expression. "Where was I? Where were you?"

"Me? I was at the skating rink—right where you told me were going."

"When did I tell you that?" Brightly scoffed. "We went to the football game. I told you we were. Beckett was playing." Her eyes became dreamy, and Saige breathed in long and deep. "You told me we were going skating, Brightly."

"Saige Pemberton, I'm telling you, I did not. Just apologize to me for ditching us. You don't have to make excuses. I can read you, you know." Brightly gave Saige a knowing look that made her instantly feel uncomfortable. "I don't know what you're talking about." Why was friendship so hard? Or was it just Saige's terrible taste in friends?

"Sure you don't, Saige." Now it was Brightly sighing in annoyance. "Well, anyhow, you coming?"

"Excuse me? Come where?" Had she just missed an entire conversation?

"Skating. Oh, Saige, surely that was the mixup. We told you we were planning to go skating today, and you thought we meant yesterday." Brightly shrugged. "You coming?"

Saige looked at her, her genuine, expectant expression.

Was it possible she had misheard Brightly yesterday?

She regarded her maybe-friend warily, wanting nothing more than to go home. "I don't know, Brightly." She caught the tone shift in her voice and tried to pull herself back together. Blowing up at Brightly wouldn't do anybody any good.

Brightly sighed, rolled her eyes, and grabbed Saige by the shoulders. "Come on, Saige."

What other answer was there to give? If she wanted

a completed schedule today, she didn't have a choice. She gritted her teeth. "Fine. I'll see you then."

As Saige trudged home from the bus stop, fists clenched inside her jacket pockets, her heart felt heavier with each step, and by the time she got home she felt ready to collapse of exhaustion.

This time of year always got to her—Testing pressure; the emphasis on withdrawals. And why the emphasis on withdrawals bothered her was something she knew she couldn't talk about. So she did what she did every spring— did her best to shove it out of her mind and go about her life like nothing was wrong.

She stepped inside her house, kicked off her shoes, then grudgingly put them back onto the rack and hung up her jacket on its hook. Her watch beeped: rest hour. She lugged her bag up to her room and dropped it on its hook before dropping herself onto her bed and pulling her favorite quilt up to her chin.

She missed Linley.

Thoughts of her current friend situation reminded her of the hollowness filling her. Time with these friends didn't leave her feeling happy or fulfilled—she came away usually frustrated or upset, and she still couldn't pinpoint exactly why. Maybe it was because unlike Linley, she didn't trust Brightly with anything. Maybe it was because also un-like Linley, Brightly didn't seem to care about her as a person.

Saige breathed in deep, curling up under her blanket. She wanted to be more than this; she knew she could be more than this shallow person she'd felt like for the past few months. She could be a better friend. A better sister. A better person overall.

Her eyes drifted shut, her mind locked on this goal.

In the few moments she slept, she saw a misty image of a small girl with brown curls like her own, proudly presenting Saige with the quilt almost too heavy for her.

"Look what I got you for your birthday, Saige!" she cried animatedly through her grin.

The quilt was aqua blue, Saige's favorite color, and had blue and green fringes.

Her watch, Purple to reflect her score from last year, dinged right at 3:55, signaling that she had five minutes left before social hour began.

She turned over on her back, pulled the quilt up under her chin, and replayed her conversation with Brightly in her mind. She still wasn't sure how she felt about it, but she might as well just give her friend another chance.

Walking down her street, she focused on the cool, relaxing breeze, the sound of the wind rustling the trees above, the voices of children laughing as they played in their yards with friends.

A young girl, maybe three or four years old, intercepted her path on the sidewalk, chasing a pink frisbee into the street. Saige watched her run after it, laughing, then turn and fling the disc back at her father, waiting in the yard, while her mother called apologetically to Saige. "I'm so sorry, honey!" she said, then, to her daughter, "Cassie, sweetie, please apologize to the nice girl you nearly ran into."

The girl glanced up at Saige for a moment, barely acknowledging her as she mumbled a rushed apology. Saige's mouth had gone dry, her body rigid and her eyes locked on the small figure as she dashed back toward her family.

Of course the name would go back on the lists; it wasn't in use anymore.

After a long moment Saige regained feeling in her legs and, ignoring the concerned glances of passersby, she walked fast as she could, away from the family, from the girl, from the name.

She arrived at the rink right as Brightly got there. Her friend squealed. "You made it!"

Saige nodded, her heart still pounding from the incident on the way here. Around her, some other friends had arrived, laughing and smiling and oblivious to her turmoil. She suddenly felt panicked; what kind of friends were they, if they couldn't even recognize when she was upset?

Marzia, one of Brightly's good friends, made a pointless joke and Saige laughed unexpectedly. It came out forced. Nobody noticed.

Inside, Saige picked up her skates, swiping her

watch at the counter to log her social hour here. Then she headed over to where her friends sat, still laughing over something probably pointless, and she stalled, second thoughts whirring through her mind. Had she made the right decision in coming today?

She stood in indecision for a moment before taking another deep breath and walking toward them. Maybe she wasn't finding the fulfillment she needed because she wasn't looking for it. She closed her eyes a minute, then slid toward them. "Who's ready?" she crowed, right as she missed a step and plunged to the floor face-first. Brightly shrieked, but more in the energy of the moment than of actual concern for her friend. Saige got to her feet, steadying herself on a bench, and forced a laugh, rubbing her face. "Like I said! Who's ready?" Her feet slid out from under her a second time and suddenly she found herself once again on the floor. This time, both Marzia and Brightly, as well as the other girls, erupted in laughter.

Usually making people laugh made Saige feel good, but today, she felt the same as ever before. And as she listened to their laughter above, it seemed suddenly that they were more laughing at her than with her.

"Alright, guys." Brightly bent down to Saige, extending her hand. "Come on, Saige. Try to actually get on the skate floor before falling again, alright?" She laughed, her tone condescending as she pulled Saige to her feet.

"Are you implying I'm going to fall again?" Saige regained her balance and took a careful step. "I'm obviously the best skater here."

Brightly rolled her eyes, but the others laughed.

All of a sudden Saige wanted to be anywhere but here.

Anywhere but here, where nobody saw through her enough to recognize she was upset. Here, where they only laughed at her expense.

She had seen these characteristics in her friends so many times before, but she had never let herself think hard on it.

Sliding along the floor, seeing the bunch of them skating up ahead, Brightly already deep into some funny story, having completely forgotten Saige, she had the sensation that she could leave right now and none of them would notice.

So she did.

The attendant at the counter gave her a strange look as she turned in her skates fifteen minutes into social hour, and then she left without looking back.

In the park, she found a bench and sat down, fighting unwanted tears as she tried to comprehend what had just happened and now, what she could possibly do with all this extra time. Her mind flashed back to last night, when her parents had scolded her for at least fifteen minutes upon finding about her blank schedule. She really didn't want to go through that again.

Eventually, she stood up and found herself wandering through the park. The grounds were full of kids and teens alike, playing sports or just hanging out and talking. In a previous time, Saige might've walked up to them and befriended them—she'd made a lot of friends that way— but she couldn't find the courage within herself now.

She stopped in the middle of the park and looked around, at all these groups of friends hanging out, all these people with friends to rely on, all these people that were surely very nice people but still didn't spare her a second glance. She couldn't even blame them. She'd never spared a second glance for those she saw alone, either. She'd always assumed they had their own friends, that they were just waiting for someone or something.

A ball sailed out of nowhere and smacked her against the side of the head. She staggered sideways, pain erupting around her ear as her hands flew up.

"I'm so sorry!" someone cried. Saige fell to the ground, eyes squeezed shut and clutching her head. Someone knelt beside her, grabbed her hand. "Are you okay? Do we need to call for help?"

She cracked open her eyes to see a girl about her age

with long blonde hair and a terrified expression on her face.

She managed to shake her head, and then tried to sit up straight. "I'm fine." She met the girl's compassionate gaze and blinked at her for a moment before standing up, wobbling a bit. The girl stood up quickly with her, too. "Are you sure you're alright?"

Saige nodded, holding her gaze. "I'm fine. I recognize you. What's your name?"

"Mirren," she said. "We have History together. You're Saige, right?"

"Yeah," Saige said, a little surprised Mirren knew her. "And right. History. You're a level ten, too, right?"

"Yes. And don't feel bad about forgetting me. I sit in the back, and I don't like to talk in class much." She shrugged, as if that explained it.

"Yep." Saige nodded slowly, rubbing her ear, then looked up to see more kids coming up behind Mirren, echoing their friend's concerns on Saige's condition. She nodded at all of them, and then said to Mirren, "You guys playing kickball or something?"

"Dodgeball, actually," a girl behind Mirren said, and came up behind Mirren to study Saige carefully. "You want to play with us? Unless you're just waiting on friends?"

Saige looked back and forth between the girl and Mirren. "Actually, I'm not," she said. "I'd love to play."

Throughout the game, Saige wracked her brain, trying to think of an instance where Brightly had been as kind to her as these girls, but she couldn't think of one time.

By the end of social hour, she was sweaty and tired, but she found that a bit of hope had sprung alive inside her: a hope that maybe, if her friendship with Brightly truly was over, she wouldn't have to be all alone during social hour after all.

Saige capped her pen and slid it into its place in her binder as she gathered up her things at the end of the school day.

She enjoyed school, and it showed—she excelled in every subject—but while she found joy in learning, she was glad for the solitude that rest hour would bring, a much-needed recharge before heading out again for social hour.

Social.

Her heart sank. She had no one for social today. There was no way she would seek Brightly out, not now. Suddenly her steps were slower, her movements smaller, as she walked out of the school. She would relax and recharge for an hour—for what? To wander the streets aimlessly, trying to fake having friends? She crossed her arms tighter against her chest.

For a moment her heart soared—maybe the girls from yesterday would be around—but just as quickly her attitude dropped back down. She knew virtually nothing about them other than their names; and she wasn't about to track them down and beg for a friendship. And even if she did know where to find them, why would they want to hang out with her? They had their own thing going already; they didn't need her.

And if trying to navigate this wasn't enough, it had to be Testing season, too.

Only a few weeks, she reminded herself as she got off the bus and walked toward her home, nestled in the middle of the row of townhomes that made up the living sections of her flawlessly operated community. She knew she shouldn't be complaining. Her community really did run flawlessly.

Only a few weeks. And all of the pressure would be behind her.

When social hour arrived, she caught her older brother, Archer, before he left.

"Arch," she said hurriedly, ignoring the wary look on his face, like he already knew exactly what she was going to say. "I—I kinda don't know have anything for social today. Can I tag along with you and your friends?" She knew it was abnormal, hanging out with a sibling for social hour; that was for family hour, later on in the evening. But it wasn't against standard, and she needed somewhere to be.

"Saige," Archer began to protest, but then he

sighed. "Fine. We're playing basketball down at the court. Is that okay with you?"

"Fine," Saige said in a second, already reaching toward the rolling storage racks for her gym shoes.

They walked briskly down the sidewalk and within seconds, Saige felt regret. What was she doing, humiliating Archer in this way? Nobody did social hour with siblings.

She shrunk back to walk behind him, but he turned, giving her a look of exasperation mixed with confusion. "What are you doing?"

"I—Archer, just go. I'll find someone else to hang out with." She shook her head, frustration mounting and reminding her of the her hopelessness.

"Who?" he pointed out. "C'mon, it's not that big of a deal, Saige. You know that. My friends won't mind."

"At least you have friends." It came out harsher than she intended, but she didn't take it back. "I'll find someone. I'm capable of talking to people."

"I know you are," he empathized as she turned and stormed away.

What was she doing?

She had found a bench to sit on and was trying to sort out her thoughts and figure out what the right thing to do was when she heard someone calling, and when she looked up, it was the girl from yesterday—Mirren.

"Hey, I know you!" she cried, sliding onto the seat next to her. "You alright?"

"What? Yeah…yeah, I'm fine," Saige stammered, blinking at her.

"Alone again?" Mirren asked, swinging her legs up to sit cross-legged and propping her head in her hands.

Saige studied her, debating whether or not to answer. "Yeah, sort of," she finally said.

"Risa and I were going to hang out at my house," Mirren said. "You want to come? Maybe we could watch a movie or something?"

Saige blinked, shocked at Mirren's invite. Her gut response was no—but as the thought processed in her mind, she found it actually a little appealing. Try something new, get to know some new friends. Wasn't this what she was just thinking she needed?

"I don't even know your family," she stalled. "I barely know you."

Mirren shrugged. "Ah, they won't care. Come on!"

She did need somewhere to be. What was there to lose, anyway? "Okay, sure."

"Awesome!" Mirren leapt up from the bench. "Let's go!"

A girl Saige recognized from the park yesterday was waiting on the sidewalk in front of Mirren's house. When she spotted them, she ran and practically jumped on Mirren. "I've been waiting! Where have you been?"

Saige felt her hope evaporate. If Mirren already had a best friend, that made Saige an unneeded asset here. As the thought process registered, she shook her head, trying to erase it. Before, she never would have cared if Mirren had a best friend already—she would have befriended her anyway. Had Brightly's influence on her life been so powerful to cause her to change so much?

"Risa," Mirren cried. "I thought you were with family today."

Saige heaved a breath, suddenly wanting to leave. So that's all she was to Mirren—someone to keep her from breaking schedule. Not an actual friend.

"Well, I thought you were going with Emory today," Risa retorted good-naturedly, crossing her arms.

"Turns out she has some event at Northside she forgot about," Mirren replied, glancing over her shoulder at Saige. "Risa, you remember Saige, right?"

self because Linley played a prank on you and left the top unscrewed."

"I remember that, too!" Risa laughed, a smile blossoming over her face. "Your expression was priceless. How did I not remember before?" She looked at Mirren. "Didn't we call her something funny for a long time, because we didn't remember her name?"

Mirren frowned in concentration, then her face lit up as she successfully recalled the hilarious memory. "Yes! You were Apple Juice Girl. Because you spilled apple juice on yourself." She looked at Saige as she said this, laughter on her lips. Saige's gaze was steady, her mind tossing as she returned a polite smile. Risa and Mirren knew her? Talked about her? Had a silly name for her? She didn't remember Linley's birthday at all. Linley had known them? She turned back to study the picture; it was probably a few years old.

"Do you remember when that was?" she asked them.

"It was a while ago," Risa said, still laughing. "Can I please call you Apple Juice Girl from now on?" she joked.

Now that Saige thought about it, maybe she did remember that party. Maybe she did remember a prank Linley played on her where she spilled her entire drink on herself. Then again, she and Linley were always playing pranks on one another. There had been so many funny ones over the years that it was hard to keep track of them all.

Wishing that she had some sort of funny response, she laughed a little at Risa's comment, and then sat down on Mirren's pink-cushioned window seat and pulled her legs up under her. If she was here, she might as well contribute something to the conversation. "Tell me about yourselves," she invited. "What do you like to do? What are your families like?"

Risa and Mirren exchanged a look—causing Saige to shift uncomfortably, feeling suddenly unwanted—and then Risa plopped down on the floor in front of Saige and said, "I just have one younger sister. Brynlee. She's eight and in the second level. My dad works in waterworks, and my mom is a community leader. She works in management of the food network."

"That's cool," Saige said, frustrated with her lame reply.

"As for what I like to do...I don't know." Risa shrugged and chewed on her lip. "I really like arts and crafts. And organizing things. I might go to High Honor for management."

"You and your brilliant mind," Mirren joked, but there was an odd underlying tone to the jest.

"My brother thought about doing management."

Saige smiled at Risa, shaking her head. "He's the most scattered person I know, though, so we all knew that wouldn't last. And of course, he's changed his mind since. I think now he's wanting to do law? Or maybe filmwork? Who knows."

"Yeah?" Risa laughed. "Who's your brother? Do I know him?"

Saige shrugged. "He's in twelfth level, so I doubt it. Archer. Archer Pemberton?"

Risa frowned, then shook her head.

"My sister's in thirteenth level," said Mirren. "Maybe she knows him." She, too, sat down and leaned back against her bed, her gaze distant. "She wants to go to Westview for High Honor."

"What?" Risa exclaimed. "I thought she was at Northside today."

"She is," Mirren said. "But she doesn't really want to go there. She's going just by technicality. She can't pick her High Honor without visiting them all." She played with a loose thread on her shirt. "Did I tell you Dawson's already talking about what ring he's getting Ashlyn?"

"What, really?" Risa shifted positions to face her friend, concern and excitement meshing on her face. Saige felt like she had become invisible to them, and she slumped lower, pulling her knees to her chest. She wanted to jump in, say something funny, be bold like she always used to be, but she couldn't find it within her.

"Yeah," Mirren said. "You should see this family

whenever he comes to visit. We're all an anxious wreck."

She scoffed half-heartedly, like she was trying to convince herself it was ridiculous to feel anxious about huge life changes. "It's their marriage year. One of these times he'll pull us aside and ask our blessing for his proposal."

Mirren made a face then resumed playing with the loose thread, twisting it and untwisting it around her finger.

She abruptly sat up straight and looked at Saige. "What about you, Saige?" she asked. "Tell us about yourself."

"Well," Saige said. Why was she so awkward today? "I have one older brother, like I said, Archer. He's been doing the whole High-Honor-touring thing lately, too. I don't know what I'll do when he leaves. I mean, I still have a year, but..." She laughed a little, regretting her words. She didn't know these girls well. She had no business dumping her personal struggles on them. What next, sharing her heartache over losing Linley?

"I like to do a lot, I guess." That much was true. "I just haven't done much of anything lately. I like sports. Fashion, sometimes. Adventures. Though I haven't been on any in a while."

"I like adventures," Mirren replied, a corner of her mouth turning up in a smile.

"You're a lot quieter than usual, Saige. Something on your mind?"

Saige looked up from the traditional Thursday dinner of soup—today, chicken noodle. "Just thinking," she said, dropping her gaze back down to her bowl. It was true, but not the whole truth—she didn't want to confess the whole truth, which was that she had found herself unexpectedly having more fun at social this afternoon with Risa and Mirren than she ever had with Brightly.

She couldn't admit it because doing so would be admitting all those times spent with Brightly had been a waste, and that she made a mistake in letting herself become swept up in that crowd.

"Oh yeah?" Archer said. "Anything interesting?" She shrugged. "Not really."

"What did you do today, Archer?" asked their father, setting his spoon down.

"Went to see the new documentary that just came out," Archer said, sipping the last of his soup. "About how we came to be. Our society."

"I've heard it's really good," Saige offered. Brightly had been talking about it for weeks.

"It was, actually," Archer said. "Someday, I'll be the one directing those films." He got up, collecting the empty soup bowls and bringing them to the sink. Saige propped her head on her hand and let her gaze wander along with her thoughts. "I thought you were going into law study."

"Are you saying I can't do both?" Archer said.

"How's reviewing going, honey?" her mother asked, interrupting. "Testing's not too far away."

Saige snapped back to focus. "Yeah, I know. I'm doing fine." She got up and went over to the sink to begin rinsing the bowls for the dishwasher.

"What's your percentage of questions correct so far?" her mom continued.

"One hundred." Saige didn't like talking about her successes. It was just something else to live up to— something else she feared would go up in smoke, just like her friendships had, just like she felt her old self had. What if her intelligence disappeared next? What would happen if she were to sit down for the test and find all her knowledge gone? She'd managed to get rid of Linley practically overnight, and now, she supposed, the same went for Brightly.

Which was why a part of her was having a hard time digesting this whole apparent new friendship with Mirren. How was she to ensure she didn't mess it up?

. . . .

Three girls spending study time together was not a combination for success, but it wasn't like Saige truly needed the practice. She had come anyway, though. Of course she had. She didn't want them to think she didn't want to spend time with them. Besides, she had figured she could possibly help them out.

"Ugghhh," Mirren groaned, sitting at Risa's desk, seeming repulsed by it. "I am not ready for testing."

"When is anyone?" Saige pointed out.

"Mirren," Risa said, sprawled on her bed writing notes in her notebook, "you score Purple every year. You have nothing to worry about." So maybe Mirren and Saige had more in common than she'd first thought.

"Not every year," said Mirren. "I got Blue two years ago."

"And that's so bad," said Risa, rolling her eyes. She shrugged and flopped back down on her stomach, looking over at her book for phrases to copy into her notebook for memorization.

"You know what we need to do sometime?" Mirren

still hadn't opened her study booklet. "Go to the Arts Center again. I have an itching to paint." She propped her chin on her hand and surveyed the room, looking like she was going to keep talking but remaining silent.

Saige was taken back to throwing paint at canvases in her backyard with Linley, and how furious her mom had been to come out and see her concrete patio stained all colors of the rainbow.

"Don't you paint every day already?" said Risa dubiously, looking up at her.

"Yeah, during rest, but that's just doodles and mindless art. I want lessons and I want to do it with you guys." Mirren twisted a piece of hair around her finger.

"We should do it," Saige said, and looked up when no one replied to see Risa studying Mirren curiously, who was still twisting her hair, more fiercely now.

Was something going on that Saige was missing? She hated tension and conflict. She held up her notebook, hoping they wouldn't notice her page was still blank. "Talk later. Risa's mom is going to think we're skipping."

It hadn't been a joke, but Mirren gasped in mock horror, turning back to the desk reluctantly. "What? She wouldn't really think that!"

Risa laughed, and Mirren looked at her in mock confusion. "What, did I do something?"

"You're distracting me is what you're doing," accused Risa, pointing at her notebook. "I'm going to forget everything I just learned."

"Apologies," said Mirren, ripping a page covered in doodles out of her notebook, "but I think this is distraction-worthy art."

"Mirren!" Risa launched off the bed and wrestled the notebook from Mirren's hand before smacking it down on the desktop. "Focus!"

"Risa!" Mirren mimicked. "Focus!"

"Whatever! I'm done with this!" Risa turned to flop back on her bed, but underestimated the distance and ended up on the floor. Saige's jaw dropped, but before she could say anything Mirren had rolled off her chair and onto the floor next to her friend, laughing and laughing and laughing.

"I hate you!" Risa exclaimed as she got up, rubbing her elbow. "I'm going downstairs!" But she only got back on the bed, crossed her arms, and fake-glared at Mirren, who couldn't stop laughing.

Saige watched the entire exchange in awe. Again that feeling of irrelevance had risen up. She wasn't needed here—they obviously had a great thing going without her—but something had changed in her as she watched, and somehow that feeling didn't predominate as it usually did.

"Saige," Archer said, stepping into her room as she braided her hair for bed. She looked at him warily as he sat on her bed. "What's new?"

She regarded him with a look of disbelief.

"Fine, whatever, don't accept your dear brother's invitation to conversation. I just wanted to make sure you remembered what Saturday was."

"Of course I do," she said without a pause, though she didn't.

"Well," he said, rubbing his hands together as he stood up. "Good. I wasn't sure if you'd still want to do it…"

Then it clicked in her mind. May 7.

Cassie's—

No. That wasn't what Archer meant; she remembered now, in an instant. Pemberton sibling day—the one day a year she and Archer set apart for just the two of them to do something together. Last year they'd gone ice skating on the then-brand-new outdoor ice rink in the park and Saige had slipped, fallen, and twisted her ankle. What had been worse was the aftermath: the wary, almost disdainful, looks of passersby whenever she came tromping down the block in the huge black cast. People rarely got physically injured, and the ice rink had been a huge controversy for that reason. After word of Saige's injury got out, it was shut down.

"This year we do something safe," she said to her brother, who fell backwards, guffawing. "Oh, stop," she scowled at him. "You wouldn't be laughing if it had been you enduring the humiliation for weeks."

"That will never be truly known, will it?" he said, getting up again. "Well, I'll be thinking of better—*safer* options for this year!"

"I don't even know why I even still do it with you!" Saige shouted after him, but he only laughed as she rolled her eyes.

● ●

The first week of May was upon them, which marked the final full week before Testing began, and as always, it revealed that everyone was in a state of mild panic.

She was in the park again, waiting for Risa and Mirren to play a game of soccer, kicking the ball around aimlessly, and accidentally sent it spiraling farther than she intended. As she went to chase after it, her eyes caught on a familiar face. Of all the times…

She picked up the ball and headed back, hoping Brightly hadn't noticed her

Grinding her teeth, she fought the anger rising within her. "Brightly Blackwell. What a coincidence to see you here." Too overdramatic? She clenched her fists at her side. *Get ahold of yourself, Saige.*

She met Brightly's eyes, challenging her. Brightly's arrogance heated the space around them. Had Saige truly never seen it before—or was it only now appearing? What had changed, Brightly or Saige's viewpoint?

"Saige Pemberton," Brightly replied, slowly and deliberately, crossing her arms and glaring at Saige. "What might you be doing at the park today?"

"Listen," Saige said, swallowing, and then shook her head quickly. "I don't know what your deal is, Brightly, but in case you didn't get the memo, I'm done hanging out with you. So if you expect me to just mindlessly follow you now that you've found me again, you can just give up on that idea right now." She crossed her arms as well.

Brightly's jaw dropped. "My deal? You're the one who quit talking to me."

Saige stared at her for a long moment, feeling lost. Did Brightly truly believe she was in the right?

Finally, she heaved a sigh, looking around to see if anyone had arrived that could save her from this. Her eyes caught on Risa and a girl she recognized as Evie, a friend of Risa's, but they were on the other side of the park. Sighing again, she turned back to Brightly. "I'm sorry, Brightly. I'm done with this. You. Our friendship."

As she spoke, she felt her stomach twist. She was doing the right thing, right? Could Brightly be right? Was Saige at fault again? But surely she couldn't be imagining the distinction she now saw—the difference between Brightly and Mirren. She had to believe that.

Brightly's idea of friendship was not the kind of friendship she wanted.

Saige closed her eyes for a minute to regain her confidence. "I'll see you later." Ball tucked under her arm, she spun away, ready to walk away from that part of her life.

Before she could even take a step, Brightly had reached out and grabbed her shoulder. "Saige."

Desperation wracked her. "What? I actually have plans today, you know." Again, her insides twisted. Did Brightly? Was she doing to Brightly exactly what Brightly had done to her—ditching her?

Brightly opened her mouth, then shut it. "Saige, are you still the..." She trailed off, and then made air quotes.

"... 'little rebel' they call you?"

Saige blinked at her, trying to make her disregard as apparent as possible. "Am I *what*?"

"Remember...your story...about how your family called you the little rebel?" Brightly's eyes were piercing, her gaze steady.

"Where are you going with this?" Saige bounced the ball on the ground once, then looked over her shoulder. "I have friends waiting."

"You first. Answer my question first."

"Brightly," Saige said wearily, "I'm sorry. I don't know how to answer you. I don't really care either way. I'll see you later." Shoving Brightly's hand off her shoulder, she turned and walked away quickly before Brightly could pull her back again.

Her mind cleared, and of course she remembered the story about the funny nickname her parents and Archer used to call her. But why would Brightly want to know—how had she phrased the question? If they still called her that? It made no sense.

Then again, like *anything* about Brightly made sense.

The game had ended and they were sitting on the bench, resting, and Risa had just gone to fill up their water bottles when Saige noticed Mirren's gray look.

"Mirren?" she said.

Mirren pulled her knees up to her chest and didn't look at Saige. Instead, she played with a frayed hem on her shirt and shrugged. "Testing's in one week," she finally said.

It was so out of context that it took Saige a minute to process it. "It'll be okay," she said after a moment, for she couldn't think of anything else. "You know you'll do fine. Didn't I once hear Risa say you were a Purple student?"

"Yeah," Mirren said, without a change of expression.

"You'll do fine," Saige said, looking at her, though Mirren wouldn't return the gaze. "And you know what, Mirren? Even if you don't do so great, I'll still be your friend. We'll all still be your friends. Nothing will change that. You know that, right?"

She was surprised by the words that came out of her mouth, but didn't take them back. Mirren turned to look at her then, her blue eyes deep and soulful, the freckles on her face standing out in the sunlight that reflected off her long blonde hair. "Thanks, Saige."

After a moment, she said abruptly, "Do you ever get nervous about Testing?"

Saige shifted positions. "Well," she said. "Who doesn't?"

Mirren propped her head in her hands, intent on her words. "You didn't answer my question."

Saige scratched her elbow, now avoiding Mirren's gaze. "I generally do really good on it, so I really shouldn't have reason to be worried."

Mirren wasn't backing down. "Yeah, well, people tell me that, too."

"Oh yeah?"

"Yeah," Mirren said, more boldly.

"Well," said Saige, rubbing her eyes as she sorted through her thoughts. When she opened her eyes, it was just in time to see Risa trip over a root and fall face first in order to avoid getting out. "Poor Risa," she laughed, but stopped when she didn't hear Mirren laughing along.

"I don't know, Mirren," she said, irritably. "Why are you pushing this?"

Mirren shrugged. "I don't know." She fingered a strand of her hair. "My older brother...Dawson...he just got engaged to Ashlyn yesterday, and I'm happy for them and all." She paused, ran a hand down her hair. "And then Emory—my sister—stood up and announced she's going to Westview for High Honor and I—" She swallowed. "I guess I'm just not ready for them to both leave me. And then Testing." She heaved a sigh, ran her fingers through her hair again and looked over at Saige. "I sometimes feel like I just …can't handle the pressure anymore."

"I know the feeling," Saige said, wondering if she was saying the right thing.

"I'm going to be all alone in the fall," Mirren said, turning around on the bench and resting her chin on her arms. "No siblings at all. I mean, yeah, sure, I'll still see Emory on the weekends, but it's not the same."

"No, probably not."

"And Dawson…he'll be building his own family, which, again, I'm excited about, but that also means he's … gone for good, I guess."

"Not for good, Mirren," Saige reminded her, noticing the way Mirren's gaze lowered as she spoke.

"You'll still see him. Your families will still get together, and you'll get to play with his kids and be that cool aunt they adore."

Mirren smiled a little. "I guess that's true."

"And Testing—Mirren, you know you'll do fine." She felt like a hypocrite, saying all these things to Mirren that she knew firsthand wouldn't help.

"I suppose." Mirren's face clouded again, and she sat upright. "How much longer is this game going to go?"

"You know," Saige said, suddenly, "I get it. That fear of Testing."

Mirren's gaze shot back at her.

"I've been a perfect scorer my entire life," Saige said. "I sometimes feel like people seem to think it's impossible for me to have nerves or anxiety. They laugh it off if I bring it up. You don't."

Mirren shrugged. "I get it. Testing's not easy for me, but I do well. People tell me I'm dumb to worry about it."

"Then I'll be dumb with you," Saige said, grinning.

"Thanks, Saige," Mirren said quietly.

"You too," Saige said. "For listening."

"Same for you," laughed Mirren in reply. On a sudden urge Saige reached over and squeezed her friend, and she was surprised by the tight hug she got in return.

⠀⠀⠀⠀•••••••••••••••••••••••••••••••••••••••⠀⠀⠀⠀

"Saige."

She heard his voice and wished she could disappear, slink back out the door. "Hi...Archer." Play it casual?

"Where did you go?" he said. "We were supposed to do Pemberton sibling day."

"Pemberton sibling day," Saige repeated, hesitantly. "Did I ever say I could?"

She avoided her brother's eyes as she hung up her coat and slipped her shoes on the rack.

"Saige," he said. "It's always this day, every year.

May 7."

"It is?" she said, already knowing her act was failing.

"Saige," he said, his voice heavy. "Just tell me you forgot."

But that wouldn't have even been the truth.

But if she answered so from the perspective of just obeying what he said, was it really lying?

"I forgot," she mumbled robotically.

"Saige," he said in a low voice.

"Why do you keep saying my name like that?" she sniveled, trying to hide her emotions.

When there was no reply, she rushed up the stairs, to her bedroom and slammed her door.

Just when she thought she had a grip on things, that she was doing something right, that she was helping some-one...she had been failing someone else.

Desperation took hold of her again, and she hated every twist of emotion within her. Was there one area of her life she *wasn't* failing at?

At lunchtime Monday, Saige pulled her lunch out of her bag, shoved her bag in her locker, and turned to go to lunch when she found herself face-to-face with Brightly.

"Brightly, I thought we'd settled this." She didn't hide the weariness in her voice. "I don't want to eat lunch with you."

"I don't want to eat with you, either." Brightly smirked as she spoke, then her eyes narrowed. "Saige, I need an answer regarding my question."

"What question? Brightly, I don't have time for this." Saige tried to shove past her, but Brightly grabbed her arm, and for a moment Saige felt a sudden, inexplicable feeling that something was off.

"Brightly, what on earth are you talking about?"

"You always loved doing rebellious things before," Brightly said, her gaze piercing. "Are you still that way?"

"*What*? Why does it matter?"

Brightly pursed her lips, then she turned and fled without a word. Saige shook her head to clear it before heading to lunch.

Testing day had an entirely different schedule than a normal day.

Saige was allowed, like all other high school students, to sleep until eight-thirty, and she was permitted twenty-five minutes to get ready, instead of twenty. After breakfast there was an hour of rest spent most certainly not resting, and then a brief family time period. As usual, Saige's parents were full of encouragement, telling Saige and Archer how they couldn't wait to see their High Purple bands.

As much as they acted like they were teasing, Saige heard the seriousness behind their words. Not because they were trying to pressure their kids, but because they genuinely believed Saige and Archer could do nothing less than the best. Which Saige knew was probably true, but somehow, the knowledge really didn't help her nerves.

Testing began at one p.m., and for high school students it would go until four. Younger levels had shorter Test periods, but at high school level they had the three full hours and five hundred questions.

Right at twelve, Saige and Archer, along with their parents, got in the line to enter the Testing building.

It was raining, and while Archer cowered under his jacket, Saige laughed and spun in the rain, letting it pour over her. She needed the welcome distraction. Her mother watched in disapproval. "Saige, don't you think you should be taking this time to prepare yourself?"

"I am." Saige gazed up at the gray clouds, unflinching as droplets splashed on her face. "I'm clearing my mind. You should try it, Archer."

He grunted and looked away. Saige scowled. He'd been like this since the day she ditched him. And she supposed he had reason. But couldn't he let it go just for one day—Testing day, no less?

"Saige, you're going to walk in there soaking wet." Her dad cleared his throat, but Saige ignored his gaze of disappointment. "We all will," she pointed out. "You forgot the umbrella."

Her parents exchanged looks of defeat. Saige just continued to spin in the rain, not caring about who was watching her.

When they reached the door, Saige felt her heart begin to pound. The building was only used for Testing, which meant entering it each year brought back a lot of strong memories of former fears of past years.

She showed her identification at the door and passed through, and as she walked down the halls to the tenth level Testing room, she looped on her testing band, the bracelet used to identify her name, grade level, and color score from the previous year. The violet was still vibrant and new from having sat in a box for the past year.

Saige wasn't one of those kids who wore their Testing bands year round.

The testing room was huge, built to accommodate desks for all the tenth level students, plus a huge gathering area in the back to wait before Tests began. The desks and chairs were set up and still roped off from admission.

"Saige!" She turned at her name to find Risa coming up to her. "Hey, Risa."

"How are you doing?" Risa fidgeted as she spoke, her hands shaking a little.

"I'm fine," Saige said. "Risa, you'll do fine. You know you will."

"I know," Risa said, shrugging. "I know. Just this room, the day...it gets to me. Ugh." She shrugged again. "I always get this nervous, but I always do fine. Ugh. I wish I could be more like you."

If only she saw inside Saige's mind, she might see that wasn't true, though right now Saige was actually feeling pretty okay. "I'm not as unaffected as I appear," she said, honestly. "Where's Mirren?"

"Somewhere around here, I don't know. Want to go find her with me?"

"Sure," Saige said, and then frowned. "Hey, last time I talked to her, she seemed super anxious. She—I mean, she usually does good on Tests, right?"

Risa looked at her for a moment. "She's fine. She's gotten purple every year I've known her. Testing always messes with her. I'm not worried."

"Um—" Saige turned around right in time to see Mirren come up from behind Risa and throw her arms around her. "Yeah, where could Mirren be?"

Risa shrieked in surprise and spun around. "What have I told you about scaring me?" she exclaimed while Mirren laughed, and Saige suddenly felt excluded, irrelevant to them and their friendship. They had their own thing—who was she to jump in and interfere with it? Irritably, she tried to shove the thought from her mind. She knew they were all friends; she couldn't seriously expect Risa and Mirren to be completely dependent on her for the friendship. Either way, she made up her mind to let it go.   She couldn't let it bother her today.

"Saige, how are you doing?" Mirren said, grinning.

"Doing better now that we found you," Saige joked and Mirren just smiled and shook her head. Saige searched the smile for signs of the anxiety she had seen formerly, but found none.

Mirren was fine, she reminded herself as they headed inside. She was still getting to know her sweet friend, after all. She probably had just been reading too deep into things.

At 12:45, the ropes were let down, and all the students filtered through, looking for their desk. Saige found hers pretty fast, toward the front where it always was, every year. She turned around and waved encouragingly at Risa and Mirren as they went their separate ways—they both were seated near the back. Risa looked a lot better, but, in contradiction with her earlier composure, Mirren now looked about ready to faint. Poor thing. Saige slid into her seat and twisted around, but she could hardly see either of her friends from her spot. Oh well. Mirren would be okay. She was Mirren, after all. Saige couldn't imagine her not doing well on the test.

Even if she didn't, it wouldn't be the end of the world, and, like she'd promised Mirren, they'd always still be friends. Nothing would change that, not now. Saige was determined to not mess up this friendship.

"Attention, students," came the announcement over

the loudspeaker, and the lights dimmed as the screen in the front of the room lit up. Saige sat erect, chills shooting up her spine. Lost in her thoughts, the true impact of today's significance hit her again—this was *Testing*.

"Please pay attention to the summary of standards and expectations for testing," the loudspeaker said again.

"There is to be no communication whatsoever with anyone, no exceptions. Do not look at anyone's pages but your own. Cheating is punishable by withdrawal.

"You will have three hours to complete five hundred questions. Three hundred will be the school assessment, divided into sections based on subject. The last two hundred will be cultural and common knowledge to test character and morality.

"You are allowed to drink from the water bottle provided to you, but no other food or drink is permitted. Once you finish, turn your test over and sign your name. We will release everyone at exactly four, so if you finish early, you are encouraged to double-check your answers for any silly mistakes. We remind you that while Purple is the goal, Blue, Green, and Yellow are not shameful, but marks of a student who is still growing.

"Students who score all five hundred questions correct will receive a score of High Purple.

"Students who score between 450 and 499 correct will receive a score of Purple.

"Students who score between 390 and 449 correct will receive a score of Blue.

"Students who score between 300 and 389 correct will receive a score of Green.

"Students who score between 250 and 299 correct will receive a score of Yellow.

"Students who score between 150 and 249 correct will receive a score of Orange, and will be required to attend classes and conform to different schedules for the duration of the summer in an attempt to resuscitate their intelligence, and they will be permitted a re-test in August.

"Students who score below 150 will receive a score of Red and their withdrawal will immediately begin processing. There are no re-tests allowed except for our grace period of Orange."

Saige breathed in and out. In and out. She could do this.

What if I screw up? What if I mess up? What if one of my friends messes up? Breathe in, breathe out. Worrying about this now wasn't going to help. She knew she would do fine. She knew her friends would do fine. They were all brilliant students and kind people.

"Students, your time begins now. Please open your test booklet and begin your Tests."

Saige took another deep breath, closed her eyes, and listened to the sound of pencils skittering across pages for a moment before opening her eyes and looking down at her own page. *Here we go.*

Saige's family sat around a table at the formal restaurant in town, eating dinner earlier than normal, as was tradition after Testing.

"How do you think you did?" Saige's father said after a long silent moment.

Saige wondered why everyone always asked that; what answer was there really to give besides "I think I did good"? And what could anyone even believe besides that, either?

So Saige said "I think I did good," and her brother echoed it, and her parents nodded, but Saige saw the worried expression that remained on her mother's face. Saige's heart twisted, and she reached over to place a hand over her mother's fist on the table. "Mom, I don't think, I know. I know I did great. I wouldn't say that if I wasn't really sure, would I?"

The relief was so plain on her face that Saige had to

fight against laughter, something that would not be appropriate for the current context. "Mom, when do Archer and I not do great?" They'd both scored Purple every year since they started. She avoided looking at her brother as she spoke. They still weren't talking, though her parents didn't need to know that.

"I know." Her mother smiled at Saige, a relieved smile that always surfaced every year after Saige's insistence that she'd done fine. It became a little redundant, but Saige supposed she'd act the same if in her mother's place. She did act the same, sometimes—becoming overly worried about herself and Archer. She remembered being an anxious wreck her first few years of Testing, but now reality had solidified, reminding her that she was a smart student, and Archer was, too, and so there was nothing to be worried about.

Cassie had never been a smart student.

Saige swallowed and picked up her menu, trying to distract her mind. For the majority of the year she became a master at avoiding memories—but Testing season always sent the barriers around such memories crumbling.

How many years had it been? She didn't want to know.

After they finished eating, they headed their separate ways—their parents to lament with other anxious parents on the block and encourage one another, and Archer to the basketball court which might as well been his house for all the time he spent there. Though Saige knew that wasn't the only reason he was going there today. Usually, he and Saige did something together after Testing.

She wished she knew how to fix things, but a part of her still didn't feel sorry for ditching him, and she hated herself for it.

She watched him go, and then sighed and went to find Risa and Mirren while fighting away the memories still rising in her mind.

At Mirren's house, Emory answered the door with about as much excitement had it been her own friend. "Hey! Risa and Mirren just left to find you! I think they're headed to the skating rink!" Did everything Emory say have to end in an exclamation mark? "I told them I'd tell you that, so they might just go there and wait for you!"

"Okay," Saige said. "Thanks, Emory."

"No problem!" she said.

Saige left, turning over the fact *they* had been looking for *her*.

Mirren was unusually quiet as they waited in line to get their skates and swipe their watches. Saige would definitely have gone through her entire entertainment budget by the end of the month, but that was what it was there for, after all.

Sitting down on the edge of the rink, Saige focused only on the laces and tying them correctly. Mirren was still quiet while Risa chattered off built-up anxiety from the long, pressuring day.

"My parents want me home by seven-thirty," Mirren said suddenly, and Risa looked at her strangely. "That's family time, Mirren, that's everyone's deadline."

"Oh, that's right. Duh." Mirren smacked herself on the forehead. "Testing stress has gotten to me. Let's go!"

She stood up easily and pulled a wobbling Risa to her feet, clearly the more experienced of the two of them. "Saige, come on!"

"I'm coming!" Saige set off after them, but the minute she stepped foot on the rink, she slipped and fell.

Apparently, nothing had changed since skating with Brightly. Risa gaped, but Mirren started laughing. "Are you okay?"

Why not play it up? Saige leaned back dramatically, a hand over her forehead. "I don't know. I may be severely injured, never to walk again." Too much?

Mirren and Risa stared at her for a moment before Mirren laughed. "I've never seen this side of you, Saige!"

Her stomach twisted for an instant—was that a good or a bad thing, for Mirren to have never seen the old Saige? She stood up, leaning against the rail. "All better."

She took a step, and this time she didn't fall. Cautiously she crept out onto the rink. "I'm doing it! Are you proud of me yet?" She flashed a dramatic smile at Mirren, then wobbled and barely caught her balance in time.

Her friend laughed. "Here." She extended her hand, and Saige grabbed it, grinning. "Of course you're a master at this. I've skated who knows how many times, and I still haven't got the hang of it."

"You'll get there. And I don't know that I'd say 'master' for sure." But she was steady on her feet, even as she guided Saige. Brightly would always offer to help Saige, but after a few seconds she'd be off on her own again, trying to catch up with the naturally skilled Marzia.

Mirren stayed with Saige, even when Risa skated on up ahead.

Her friends couldn't keep her mind distracted forever. After a few times around the rink, Saige told them she needed a drink and got off. She was seeing Cassie everywhere again, and she was sick of it.

She stumbled her way to the water dispenser and filled a cup. Her gaze drifted back to the rink in time to see Risa and Mirren skate by, and she smiled.

She needed to get her act together. They were probably sick of all her drama. Though, her mind reminded her, she hadn't actually talked about it yet. Though in theory that wouldn't stop them from knowing something existed.

She lingered, not wanting to go back out on the rink. She could still vividly remember the last time she came here with Cassie. She found a bench and sat down, trying desperately to clear her thoughts enough to get back on the rink. But now every time she looked up she saw her sister.

Maybe a breath of fresh air would clear her mind. Leaving the building, she plopped down on a bench outside, staring into nothingness, trying to keep her thoughts focused on nothing in particular and failing.

She heard the door swing open, and then, "Hey, Saige," Mirren said, sliding to a stop and sitting down next to her, and Saige looked up at the quizzical, worried look in her friend's eyes.

Her friend, who was dealing with her own amount of anxiety, had stopped her day to come check on Saige. She had noticed when Saige disappeared. Brightly never had.

I'm fine, if that's what you're asking. It was the answer she should give. It wasn't fair to Mirren to put more on her plate.

It was the answer Saige meant to give, but when she opened her mouth, her throat had closed up and she stared at the ground, closing her eyes against the pressure building there—she just had to hold on, just a little bit longer—

"It's my sister, Cassie," she whispered, choking over her own words. "She was withdrawn in First Level. She scored Red."

Mirren stilled next to her.

Saige pulled her knees close to her chest and stared straight ahead. Her voice wobbled, and she hated it.

"We...we were all so excited when she was born. My parents had only thought they'd ever have two kids. Archer and I. I was six, Archer was seven, and Mirren...we were so excited to have a little sister. We used to spend the entire family time hour debating names we liked." Her laugh was short. "Archer found the name Archana on a list somewhere and had his heart set on it for her. You should have seen us when she was born. May 7. We were over the moon. I started screaming when my dad came with the news she was here. I just couldn't wait." Another short laugh, though this time it lingered longer. "Cassie Grace Pemberton. We doted on her."

Mirren's gaze was steady. "Go on," she said.

Saige couldn't stop talking. "She was the cutest thing ever, and she looked just like me, too, or so everyone said." A smile halfway lit up her face, but then it darkened.

"When...she started...preschool, she had a lot of trouble learning letters and numbers. We...didn't really think much of it. We used to make such a joke of it she started purposely messing up her counting or misreading things, just to make us laugh. She was hilarious."

"She sounds like you," Mirren said, gently.

"She honestly was," Saige said slowly. "Of course I never said so...you know. But she really was. She loved making people laugh. She'd make a mess everywhere, just to get attention. My mom would get so annoyed with her antics all the time, but that never stopped her." She took a shaky breath in, and the words continued rushing out of her in pace with her racing heart. "She was just so much fun, Mirren...

"When she started First Level, she didn't do well at all. Her teacher would explain something three times and she still wouldn't understand. We got her a tutor halfway through the year, and that helped a bit, but not much. She just couldn't—understand basic math facts and she couldn't read the simplest words. I can remember my mom sitting with her during relax period, going over the words on her First Level reading list again and again, and again and again Cassie would look down at the words with this flummoxed look on her face and ask, 'Show me again?'

"She wanted to learn so badly. I mean, she was fantastic in other areas...her creativity was through the roof...but that didn't matter, not in the end...not when it came to school.

"Her second-level year we started getting notices in the mail...notices that warned us she was scoring as well as a Red-level student and we should think about looking into more complex programs to help her.

"So of course we did...we looked into the programs. My parents totally freaked when the first notice came. I still remember the day, Mirren. Cassie started bawling. She was so scared." Saige was messing up the order of events a bit, but she couldn't think clearly. She swallowed again, and squeezed her eyes shut against the bitter tears clouding her vision. "My parents enrolled her in what were basically orange-classes but weren't called that..."

"Lower Level Academic Boost," whispered Mirren with a tremor in her voice, as if she were reciting something, and Saige nodded wordlessly. "And for a little while she was doing a lot better. It helped. It really did. But it was timed all wrong." Hot tears, rising in her eyes. Saige hated every tear that leaked down her cheeks. "Testing came up, and she had barely been in the program a month. There'd been a lot of progress, but just...not...enough."

She hid her face in her knees but couldn't stop talking, her voice muffled. "She came home from Testing— she was so proud of herself. It was her first, and she was just sure she did great. She kept talking about how the extra classes had taught her so much and before she would have been worried, but now she knew she was fine. She was so mature about it for a six-year-old, even acknowledging she might not have gotten the highest score but knowing she didn't do awful. And we all believed her. Why wouldn't we?" Saige's sob broke her voice, and her words fell away, succumbing to her tears as she shook.

How old was Cassie now? How long had it been, anyway? Saige had been eleven, Cassie six...and now Saige was fifteen. That made Cassie...ten.

Her sister was ten years old now.

What was she like? What did she look like?

She sobbed into her knees over questions she'd never get answers to. Somewhere out there was her ten-year-old sister, and she'd never see her again.

It was as if she had been transported back in time to that day they said goodbye and Saige dropped her speech, printed out on the page, to the floor, publicly letting go of Cassie. Telling the community they were right. Acknowledging Cassie was unfit for their community and that she was letting it all go, doing the right thing. She couldn't remember something ever being harder since.

Transported back, before that, to the moment Cassie's score was read off, and seeing the look of fear cross her sister's face, feeling her arms wrap around Saige's waist and squeeze as if holding on for her life—seeing the terror and fear fill her dark eyes—

Saige took a deep breath in, her face still buried in her knees, never wanting to lift her face, and desperately tried to calm herself down. Who did she think she was, crying in a public place over something she should have put behind her years ago? There was nothing to be done now.

She felt weak and pathetic—like a criminal, even— for breaking down in such obvious contradictions of the standards she was supposed to follow.

She was aware of Mirren wrapping her arms around her and squeezing her, but she didn't react or lift her face. She expected Mirren to leave after a few minutes when she didn't respond, but her friend didn't move either.

When a good amount of time had ticked by and she felt she could walk home, she gathered what she could of herself and sat up straight. Again she was aware of Mirren looking at her, but she didn't look back. Instead, she stood up, mumbling something about needing to get home, and left without looking back. Mirren didn't follow, but that was somehow okay.

may, year 99 | **11**

Two weeks after Testing, they got their scores back. They boarded the bus to make the same route they'd taken to get to Testing, except this time their destination was next to the Testing Center, the open arena where scores would be announced.

For some reason, Saige found herself hardly anxious at all. Archer was confident, too, and between the two of them, their parents began teasing it was as if neither had even taken the test, though Saige sensed the hidden worry still present underneath the laughter.

"Mom," Saige said, for what felt like the hundredth time, "you know Archer and I did fine."

"I know," her mom said, but the anxiety didn't leave her eyes. It never fully did, until the scores were read off. Saige stood closer to her in the line as they waited for their turn.

Mirren was up ahead a bit, and she caught Saige's eye and waved. Saige waved back, and then turned to her parents. "Would it be okay if I went and stood with Mirren to hear her score?"

"That's fine," her dad said after a minute, and Saige raced up to her friend. "Hey!"

"Hey!" Mirren lit up when she saw Saige and wrapped her in a quick hug. "How's it going?"

"Good for now, how about you?"

"I'm fine," Mirren said, too quickly, and Saige recognized the flash of anxiety in her friend's eyes.

"Remember what I told you, Mirren," she said, encouragingly, looking at Mirren in the eye. "Even if you don't do so great—"

"Mirren Rebekah Chase," called the announcer, and Saige and Mirren both jumped, not realizing she was next. Sending Saige a nervous smile, Mirren stepped forward and took a deep breath while the announcer called her stats.

"Mirren Rebekah Chase. Level: Ten. Questions correct: 210. Score: Orange."

Mirren's slight frame went so pale, and she trembled so hard, she looked like she was about to fade away. Saige's mind twisted so hard she couldn't understand what had just been said, she couldn't think—not Mirren?

Mirren's family, silent in horror and shame, surrounded her, taking her, sobbing, out of the pitying public eye. Saige had to go, had to find her family, her spot in line. But she felt she couldn't move.

"—I'll still be your friend, Mirren."

But her words were barely a breath, and Mirren was too far away to hear her heartbroken promise.

Saige received a High Purple score. But even as the announcer called off her name, she only heard it distantly, as if through a haze. It didn't matter to her anymore.

If Mirren didn't improve by the end of summer— she would be gone. Forever.

When there was a knock on Saige's door Saturday, Mirren was absolutely the last person she expected to see.

She stood in the doorway for a second before launching forward to wrap Mirren in a hug. "Aren't you supposed to be in classes?" Was something wrong?

"Not on weekends." Mirren offered a small smile. "I've missed you a lot."

It had only been a week since scores were announced, but still—"I missed you, too," Saige replied.

"Want to hang out or something?" Mirren said, not meeting her gaze.

"Sure, of course," Saige said, immediately. "Want to go find Risa?"

Mirren still wouldn't meet her eyes. "No," she said. "Not today."

They were sitting in Laikynn's, eating ice cream and having a perfectly normal conversation about favorite flavors, when suddenly Mirren went gray.

"My life is falling apart," she said, her voice quivering, her eyes locked on the melting treat in her hands.

Immediately Saige reached out and grabbed her other hand. "Mirren, look at me." Why did she sound more panicked than Mirren did?

"No one in my family has spoken a *word* to me since my score." Her voice edged on hysterical, and it frightened Saige; she had never seen this side of Mirren.

"*Mirren*. You're going to be—it's going to be fine." Where were words when she needed them? Saige's stomach twisted at the agonized look on her friend's face, and she tried again. "Mirren, I don't know what happened at Testing. Maybe you even don't. But it'll be over soon. You and I both know whatever fluke it was that caused you to score so low, it won't happen again. You're brilliant, Mirren! Everyone knows you are. It might be a rough summer, but that's all it'll be—one summer. And then everything goes back to normal." She held Mirren's gaze, pleading with her to understand, to believe.

Mirren broke the gaze and rubbed her eyes, unconvinced, and didn't say anything for a long time.

Saige watched her friend, helplessness threatening to descend. Why wasn't she more eloquent?

Finally, Mirren heaved a sigh and sat back in her chair, staring at her melted ice cream on the tabletop. "I'm sorry, Saige."

"For what?"

"Just—being like this, I guess." She grabbed a napkin and began slowly mopping up the mess.

"Being like what?" Saige said, slowly. "Genuine? Mirren, you have the complete right to be upset about this. You just can't let it defeat you."

Mirren didn't reply. She stared out the window, still half-mopping up the ice cream.

Saige shifted in her seat, her heart pounding as she watched her friend who still wouldn't meet her eyes. She didn't know how to be a friend to Mirren. She'd never had a friend confide in her like this. How was she to know she was doing the right thing?

"I just—haven't felt like myself since—you know. My score."

And suddenly, Saige knew what to say. She waited until Mirren finally looked back at her, and then she said, "Mirren, you may not be a Purple student to the world...but you'll always be a Purple friend to me. You're smart, but you're also kind, caring, and loving...and isn't that what really matters?"

Mirren swallowed, and the anguish in her eyes sent fear shooting through Saige, for she recognized the look from when she'd seen in her sister's eyes, long ago.

• •

Saige settled on the couch for family time, pulling her knees up to her chest as she waited for the rest of the family to sit down. For the first time in years she was keenly aware of the missing family member and it jolted her.

For years she had spent her life ignoring the emotions and pushing away the pain of the knowledge that her sister was gone. But seeing the familiar anxiety manifest itself in her friend was resurrecting memories she'd hoped she'd forgotten and reviving fears she hoped to never feel again. It felt as if a wall in her mind had been broken down and now the thoughts, the memories, the fears, and the emotions were running wild in her mind.

Cassie would be ten years old now. What would her life be like, having a ten-year-old sister? What would this family time be like now? What would Cassie be like? Would she be more outgoing, like Saige, or more reserved, like Archer?

"Saige, you look like you're in another world," her mother said good-naturedly as she sat down on the other end of the couch. Saige looked up warily, confusion painting her features. "What? Oh—just thinking."

"Anything in particular?" her father invited.

This circle—this time—this family—it was supposed to be her safe place. A time of intimacy, of confidence, of trust. And yet even here Saige couldn't share what was really on her mind.

"What about you guys?" she asked instead, swallowing back all the thoughts trying to escape. "How was your day? Archer?" Her voice faded at the end of his name. He didn't even look at her as he replied, instead addressing their parents as he recounted the events of his day.

As Saige watched him talk, she fought the feeling of hopelessness threatening to descend. Had it really been that big of a deal, missing their day together? She had only ever seen it as something of relative importance, something they did together just for fun.

But clearly it had been of utmost importance to her brother. And she'd just discarded it, discarded him, like it was of no worth to her.

Was there anything she didn't mess up?

"Archer," she said, her voice squeaking a bit, once family time had ended and her parents had gone upstairs. Not because she didn't want her parents to hear, because she knew they'd find out, but because this was something she needed to say to just Archer, without an audience. Her brother turned, a wary look on his face. "What, Saige?"

She suddenly felt choked up, and tugged her sweater tighter over her shoulders. "I just wanted to say I'm—I'm sorry. I'm sorry for ditching you on—you know. Sibling day. I don't know why I did. I—I shouldn't have."

His expression softened as she spoke. "Thanks, Saige." His voice was gentle, and Saige felt like collapsing in relief. "I won't do it again," she said quickly. "I promise." An idea popped into her mind. "Can I make it up to you? Can we do our day like tomorrow? Or next weekend?"

"Tomorrow would be perfect," he said, with a hint of a smile on his face.

They strolled the streets, brother and sister, sipping smoothies—their favorite—and basking in the warm summer air.

"This is really nice," Saige said, and Archer looked at her for a moment before nodding.

An urge seized Saige, and before she had the chance to stop herself, she blurted, "Archer, do you remember when we used to take Cassie to Laikynn's for ice cream?"

The air around them stilled; Saige felt a chill and looked around, fearing suddenly that someone overheard her, and then looked back at Archer, scared of his reaction, but his face had taken on an odd expression.

"Correction." He looked at her out of the corner of his eye. "I brought you two here. You were too young to go out on your own."

"Right," Saige said.

"Of course I remember," he said, his voice quieter. "She always wanted chocolate ice cream."

"Arch, you know we could get in trouble for talking about her." Her voice wavered, and suddenly, she regretted bringing it up at all.

"We're supposed to be past this," he agreed, his gaze distant.

We're. So Saige wasn't the only one in her family who felt this way?

"I think everyone who—goes through something like this feels this way for a long time," he said, still not looking at her. "They just don't act like it. Like we've done our entire lives."

Saige was still having trouble comprehending that all along, her brother had felt the exact same way.

"We have become a society fluent in lies," he said, very quietly so only Saige could hear. Walking again, she began to feel a little better, a little calmer.

"What do you think, sister?" Archer said, stopping as they waited for a city bus to pass. "Call it a day?"

"Yeah," Saige said, looking instinctively at her watch. "Social's almost over, anyway."

"Sounds good," he said.

"Archer," she said, "I'm sorry again. For all that happened."

"All good, Saige," he said, and the words lifted a weight off her chest she had forgotten was there.

Halfway home, she heard her name, and spun around to see Brightly running towards her.

She closed her eyes and stifled a groan as all the lightheartedness evaporated. She stood erect as Brightly reached her. "What do you want, Brightly?"

"Saige," panted Brightly. "I've been wanting to talk to you."

Crossing her arms, Saige listened with narrowed eyes as Brightly continued talking. "Once upon a time, Saige, you told me a funny story," she said, looking closely at Saige. How had she ever gotten along with Brightly?

"Oh yeah? I probably told you a hundred funny stories."

"The one about your name," Brightly urged, her

eyes flickering.

Saige gave her a long, exasperated look. "If you're looking for entertainment, go to the theater or something."

"You told me about how when you were born, your parents hadn't double-checked the name lists." Saige turned and started walking, not caring about being rude, but Brightly kept up. Where had Archer gone? Where was her older brother when she needed him?

"You know. How they had picked out your name, spelled the way it is, you know—S-A-I-G-E. But they didn't realize the approved spelling was S-A-G-E. And since it's such a small infraction, and nobody ever looks for that, it got completely missed."

Saige stopped walking and heaved a huge sigh to make sure Brightly knew she did not want to be having this conversation. She was also starting to wonder how Brightly remembered, almost word-for-word, a story she must've told her once.

"So nobody caught it until you were four, when you were enrolled in preschool. And by then it was too late to change it, so instead they had to change the lists, making the approved spelling your way."

Saige waited expectantly, tapping her foot.

"And you told me this to tell me how you've always been a little rebel, ever since you were born."

"What does this have to do with anything?" Saige

said, losing patience. "So what? My family used to call me 'the little rebel' in joke when I was young, but so what? It's not necessarily a nickname I'm trying to hold onto."

Brightly looked around. "Let's find someplace quieter. Come on." She grabbed Saige's arm, and again, Saige got the sense something was off. Shaking off Brightly's hand, she shook her head. "No way. Spit it out here or not at all."

"Come on, Saige, I really need your help!" Brightly looked at her with imploring eyes. "We need one more person, and I just thought my best friend would help me out." Her voice softened. "I know we've been at odds lately, but does that really ruin a whole year of good times together?"

No, but I wouldn't necessarily call all those memories "good times" anymore. Saige swallowed, hard. "I'm not your best friend, Brightly, and I'm not helping you." Something twitched within her. Could Brightly be genuine? But then why all the weird behavior lately? No, something was definitely off here.

Saige needed to leave. She spotted her brother up ahead, looking at her confusedly. Trying to somehow send the message she needed him to come back and save her, she returned the look, but he didn't get the memo. Biting her lip, Saige turned back to Brightly, who of course was talking again.

"I just want to know what happened to that little

rebel," Brightly said, quieter. "You don't seem like that at all anymore. You've changed a lot."

Saige's stomach squirmed. "I don't know, Brightly. Maybe I like my new self better." She needed to end this conversation. "Listen, I—"

"I just had an idea for you, Saige," Brightly said straightforwardly. "To be that little rebel again."

This was starting to become seriously uncomfortable. "Just give up then, Brightly, because whatever it is, I'm not doing it."

Brightly's expression became darker, challenging. Saige couldn't take this. "I don't care!" she exclaimed. "Just leave me alone. I'm not interested." She glared at Brightly pointedly.

"Fine." All gentleness gone, Brightly smirked. "I'll find someone else, then." And she disappeared.

Like she thought that would make Saige change her mind? She shook off the weird feeling. "Archer?!"

Saige pounded confidently on Mirren's door, ready to give her friend one good afternoon in the midst of her suddenly chaotic life.

Mirren perked up a little bit when she opened the door. "You have good timing. I just got home."

"Awesome." Saige bounced the ball she'd brought with on the front step. "Want to come play dodgeball? I got a bunch of us together. Thought it could be fun."

Mirren's eyes lit up, a rare sight lately, and in turn so did Saige's. "Let me just grab my shoes."

Saige waited while Mirren ran to find them. And maybe putting Risa and Mirren in the same environment would help her figure out what exactly was going on between them—why Mirren had been so against hanging out with her the other day.

Saige was the first one who got out.

"Ooh, we got the sports star out!" Evie, Risa's friend, squealed, and Saige groaned loudly as she turned to leave the playing field. "Who said I was the sports star?"

"Um, have you forgotten?" Evie called, gripping a ball in her hands and scanning for her next target. "We played volleyball together in seventh level."

Right. "Okay, so maybe I'm a little good," Saige hollered back.

"Apparently not," shouted Evie, hurling her ball at Mirren, who ducked just in time, "because you just got out first!"

"Maybe I'm having a bad day," challenged Saige, dawdling in the field. "Maybe you distracted me!"

"Me?" Evie dove to the ground to miss a ball flying at her from her brother, Easton, who had also come to play, and Saige laughed loudly and obnoxiously. "What did I do?" Evie cried.

"Evie! Saige!" Easton shouted, exasperated. "We're trying to play a game."

"Yeah, Saige!" Mirren called, grinning, "get off the field and let us play in peace!"

"Yeah, because I just mess up your game so effortlessly!" cried Saige back.

"How could you mess up our game?" called Risa. "You're the sports star!" Saige found a spot on a park bench where she was close enough to scream ridiculous commentary at the game but far enough away that she was not technically on the playing field. She felt like she had never had more fun in her life.

"And there goes Risa and—wow, that was an epic fail. What do you have to say for yourself, Dobbin?"

"Be quiet, Saige!" yelled Risa, standing up from her fall.

"Ooh, and Dobbin's anger has been sparked. What do you think, ladies and gentlemen?" Saige dramatically addressed an imaginary audience. "Will her undue frustration with the reliable commentator cost her her spot in the game?"

Risa groaned loudly, chucked a ball at Mirren and missed.

"Apparently it has cost her her throwing skills," yelled Saige, then sighed and leaned back. Her eye caught on Mirren, coming to crouch by a tree near her. "You must hate me so much, but I don't even care," she said.

"Good for you," Mirren said, rolling her eyes before returning to scanning the field for stray balls or ball-wielding players.

"This is actually really relaxing and nice," Saige said. Mirren turned to fake-glare at her, hardly containing a laugh, and Saige smiled sweetly as a ball sailed right between them. Mirren shrieked and ducked just in time before taking off in the other direction. "I will get you out, Easton!"

Saige fell off the bench laughing. She heard Mirren laugh, too, and it filled her with joy: this was what she had been hoping for—to give her friend one day she could forget about the Orange score and just play.

"Arrghh!" screamed Mirren, trying to mask her laughter with mock anger and failing. Easton hollered, "Keep it up, Saige!"

"Saige!" yelled Risa. "Stop interrupting our game!"

"Never!" Saige screamed back.

Mirren stood up in front of Saige, tone accusing, though the smile on her face giving away that she was joking. "You're having way too much fun with this. We should make you get back in the game."

"Me? The sports star, play? It'd be an honor." Mirren looked at her for a long moment, during which Saige maintained an innocent look long enough for Evie to creep up behind Mirren and tag her out. Mirren turned and screamed at her. "*Evelyn Ophelia Huntley!*"

Saige grinned, watching her, and a sudden sense of confidence filled her up. It was going to be okay.

The feeling of euphoria on Saige's part only increased when, the next day, Mirren showed up again, this time a sparkle in her eyes as she handed Saige a delicate white envelope. "Look, look!"

"What is this?" Saige fingered the elegant envelope as pieces slid together. Awestruck, she slowly looked up at Mirren's eager face. "You invited me to your brother's wedding? Mirren, don't you only get one invite?" She slid out the white cardstock and ran her finger over it.

"Yes!" Mirren said, her voice animated. "Please tell me you'll come." She clasped her hands together and tried to look pleading. Saige laughed, sliding the invite back in its envelope. "Of course I'm coming!" She bit back the next words on her tongue—for if Mirren only got one invite, how on earth did she get it and not Risa?

Dawson and Ashlyn's wedding was gorgeous. Saige walked into the community wedding room and turned in a full circle, marveling at the way it was decorated just so, with the beautiful magenta and blue hues. Dawson and Ashlyn had gone all out, and it had really paid off. Saige grinned. She loved weddings, but it'd been a long time since she'd attended one.

Smoothing down her formal dress, she found her assigned seat toward the front, near where the bridesmaids would stand. She felt a laugh creeping within her. She knew Mirren must have been involved with the wedding plans, and it was not a coincidence she was sitting so close to where Mirren would be standing.

Something bit at her inside, reminding her that maybe it wasn't intentional—hadn't this invite originally been intended for Risa? She shook away the thoughts. She didn't want to deal with worrying about that now; today, she decided, her only mission was to have fun and make sure Mirren did, too.

The ceremony was just as beautiful as the room it took place in, and despite not knowing either Dawson or Ashlyn all that well, Saige felt the joy filling the room around her. It was not only the joy for the newly-weds that Saige felt but also the joy of friendship—during the ceremony, she and Mirren had been making weird faces at each other in split-second moments when they thought nobody was looking.

She had spent so much time trying to get back her old self, but now she began to wonder if, like she'd told Brightly that one time in a moment of passion, she wasn't indeed coming to like her new self better. Though she still wasn't entirely sure what that meant.

After the wedding party had scurried out to take pictures, the guests were encouraged to make their way to the reception area for refreshments and to take some time to write kind notes to the bride and groom. Saige stole several note cards, found a corner, and wrote all of them to Mirren except one she wrote out of courtesy to Dawson and Ashlyn.

Mirren, you looked gorgeous up there! Not that you aren't gorgeous already. -Saige

Mirren, more people looked strange at me than you when we were making weird faces at each other. I'm just that much cooler.

Guess who's writing this?

I'm wasting your brother's cards. Will he be mad? I bet he bought thousands. It'll be fine. We can always recycle these.

If you don't laugh when you read these, I have failed as a best friend, so you better laugh.

Did you notice how I don't even put my name on these anymore? Guess that's one of the perks of best friends. Signatures aren't needed.

You do know who this is, right? Just compare the handwriting.

Tell Dawson and Ashlyn they are the CUTEST couple EVER!!!

Then,

I'm trying to be a better friend to you. I'm always here if you need anything. I want you to know I love being your friend more than almost anything. Thank you for being mine.

She sat back, looking at her stack of goofy notes to her friend, and felt a well inside of her fill up slowly. Even if Mirren wasn't feeling great underneath, Saige was going to make it her mission to get her through the summer. And it was already over halfway done.

It was going to be okay.

At her name, Saige swiveled around, abandoned her dinner and jumped up. "Mirren! Where you've been? You invite me and then you avoid me. Super smooth." But she was smiling and laughing.

"Well, sorry," Mirren laughed, "being a bridesmaid, it turns out, isn't all fun and games. But I'm here now." She spun in her dress. "Isn't it so beautiful? I want to wear it every day."

"It's gorgeous," Saige agreed. "This whole wedding is. Dawson and Ashlyn are so cute together."

"Oh my goodness, agreed," said Mirren, and something flashed through her eyes for a moment before the light returned. "Want to come get some cake with me?"

"Nothing I'd rather do," Saige exclaimed. Mirren grabbed her hand and dragged her through the crowd to the table piled with food. Her friend stuck a plate in her hands and took another for herself. "Let's go find a corner or somewhere quiet," she said. "I'm wearing thin of this chaos."

"Though in about ten minutes, I'm betting I have you out on the dance floor," Saige said slyly, and Mirren laughed. "Okay, fine. But I at least need my ten minutes. Want to sit outside on the steps?"

"Sure," Saige said, swiping a finger through the frosting and sticking it in her mouth. Mirren rolled her eyes at her, but it was in a good-natured way.

The heavy door thumped shut behind them as they settled on the concrete steps outside, still covered in the soft white carpet Ashlyn had walked down. The evening sky was ablaze with stars, the city streets bustling with activity as always, full of families coming and going, parents laughing, kids with sticky fingers eating cold treats. Saige smiled, just taking it in as she savored the sugary cake on her tongue.

Mirren, next to her, had gone quiet again, picking at her cake instead of eating it. Saige looked at her oddly. How was she so animated one minute and so silent the next?

She licked the frosting off her fork while looking at her friend carefully out of the corner of her eye, waiting for her to speak.

When she didn't, Saige took a breath and set her plate and fork down on her lap. "You'll still see Dawson, you know."

"Oh, I know." But there was no confidence in her words. "Emory's leaving next month for High Honor. I'll be the only one left."

"Is that really what's bothering you?" Saige regretted her words the minute they left her mouth. Did she seriously not understand the concept of giving her friend space? Familiar self-criticism descended upon her. Here she went again, traveling the path to destroying more things that were important to her.

But Mirren didn't react the way she feared. Instead, she put her plate down on the step next to her and started crying.

"Mirren!" Why did she never know what to say in these circumstances? "Mirren, what's wrong?"

"I don't know," Mirren choked out, her face in her hands. "I just don't know."

Saige searched for words, then reached out to pull her friend in an awkward hug. Mirren didn't react. When Saige pulled away, she turned to look at her, the light from around them illuminating the tears in her eyes. "Saige, what if the classes don't work?"

"What?" Saige blinked at her.

"These classes I'm taking—for my score. The orange classes. The ones supposed to fix me. What if they don't work?" More tears escaped, but she didn't wipe them away or try to hide them, but instead kept her gaze steady, as if everything in her was calling out for help.

"Mirren, that's ridiculous." Saige tried to make her own tone sound confident, brave, instead of as scared as she felt. "You're a brilliant student."

"Yeah, but I failed once," Mirren lisped. "It could happen again."

Saige put her hand on Mirren's shoulder to make sure Mirren was looking at her. "Except it won't," she said, firmly, using all her strength to keep the wobble from her voice. But why would her voice be wobbling? Mirren was just fearful, emotional, worked up. Realistically, Saige knew she'd be fine. Wouldn't she? "You are going to be just fine."

"But what if I'm not?" Desperation crept into her voice, and it meshed into anger. "You promised you'd be my friend even if my score was low, Saige, and you held fast to that. But can you really make that promise to someone who gets withdrawn? You can't, Saige. Withdrawal is the end of the story." Her words were pointed, but they lost their punch as she trailed off. She dropped Saige's gaze and wrapped her arms around herself, shaking.

Saige opened her mouth, closed it. Then she said, "Maybe I can't promise that, Mirren. But I could promise to be your friend until the last minute."

But even the promise felt weak and empty.

mirren | PART 3

7:00 Rise
          Get Dressed   (2 min)
          Brush Teeth   (2 min)
          Wash Face   (1 min)
          Tidy Room   (3 min)
          Hairstyle   (4 min)
7:15 Breakfast
7:45 Cleanup
8:05 Depart
8:15 Classes Commence
12:15 Lunch Break
12:45 Classes Resume
5:45 Depart
6:00 Dinner
6:30 Cleanup
7:00 Study
8:30 Shower
9:00 Prepare for Bed
          Pajamas on   (3 minutes)
          Brush teeth/wash face   (4 minutes)
          Clean room   (7 minutes)
          Hairstyle   (5 minutes)
9:30 Quiet Time
10:00 Bed

Sure—Mirren would openly tell anyone who asked that all this anxiety had all exploded with her low score; or even before that, on the day she realized she was losing both her siblings. And while both those played a part in her turmoil, no doubt, she knew in her heart it had first shown up long before.

It had started in First Level—the first time she scored Orange, the time when she had only scored Green at her re-test at the end of the summer, that summer full of fear and anxiety, when she was convinced she wasn't going to make it.

And since then, it felt like she was playing a wild game of trying desperately to do the right thing always and never, ever break schedule or standard, because if she did, they might look into her background and discover her score and decide it just wasn't worth it and withdraw her immediately. It was the fear that all along she had never been good enough, worthy enough, that this was all just a huge mistake and they should have withdrawn her in first level and she had barely slipped by somehow—it was that fear that bound her.

Growing up Mirren had never thought there'd be a day when she'd be so excited to see a sibling, but now, Saturdays had become something to look forward to, solely because of Dawson's visit home.

So she supposed she wasn't entirely correct, going around saying she was losing both her siblings. Dawson was already gone at High Honor, and she still saw him often enough; surely it'd be the same scenario with Emory. But soon Dawson would be married, and once he did, she'd hardly see him at all; he'd be building his own family. And with Emory also leaving, that'd leave her with no one left at all during week, even if Em visited on weekends.

It'd be different. And the knowledge of that difference was what kept her tossing and turning in bed at night, pretending like she was fine.

· ·

At the end of relax period, a knock on the front door jolted Mirren from her half-sleep state, and she sat up groggily, already feeling panic seep through her bones; she wasn't ready for visitors yet! A glance at the clock on the wall and she sighed in relief—it wasn't yet six yet, not even five-forty-five. She could easily spend five minutes getting ready without defying schedule. Dawson and Ashlyn—his soon-to-be-fiancée—must have volunteered to come for dinner preparation.

Mirren twisted her hair into her favorite style, a side braid—Saturdays meant no designated hairstyle—then brushed her teeth and splashed some water on her face before heading downstairs.

"Look who it is!" Ashlyn, bright and peppy, greeted Mirren, as always, with a tight hug. "How are you?"

"I'm fine," Mirren said, smiling back at her. "You?"

"Absolutely fantastic." Ashlyn probably didn't know how to frown. Her thin red hair hung short, just above her shoulders, a symbol of her status as a High Honor student.

Mirren blinked, realizing that meant soon Emory would be cutting off her long locks. It felt like just yesterday she had been teaching Mirren how to braid using her own long curls as an example; how had time gone so fast?

"Dawson," Ashlyn groaned, turning her attention back to Mirren's brother, who was leaning against a dining-room chair as he watched their greeting. "Are you even going to acknowledge your sister?"

Dawson rolled his eyes at her, but in a good- natured way, and then nodded at Mirren. "Hello, Mirren," he said half-sarcastically, before taking Ashlyn's hand and turning towards the kitchen.

Mirren returned the gesture half sarcastically, wondering how she could be so worked up over his leaving, and at the same time he could be so indifferent to seeing her.

"The difference in enthusiasm in those exchanges is startling," Emory said from the other room, as usual speaking what was on everyone's minds.

"I know," Dawson said, looking back over his shoulder at Mirren as he headed into the kitchen. "I'm obviously so much more involved in this relationship."

Mirren rolled her eyes. "Obviously."

"Awww, there's my sassy little sister."

"Oh, I just wonder where I got my sass from? Couldn't be Ashlyn, because I just met her last year." She couldn't keep the smile off her face. Not only was Ashlyn the opposite of all things sarcastic, but she often fought to keep the levels of sarcasm down. The comparison was so funny Mirren couldn't keep a laugh down, even when Ashlyn looked at her in genuine confusion.

"She's messing with you, Ash," hollered Emory, "but it's okay. She's only like this seven days a week."

Mirren smiled a little at Emory across the room, debated responding and decided against it. Instead, she began helping her mother with the salad for dinner.

"You have a crazy family," Ashlyn remarked, coming into the kitchen, too.

"We have an awesome family," Dawson corrected.

"An amazing family," exclaimed Emory.

As Mirren mindlessly sliced tomatoes at the counter, suddenly the feeling of love and companionship that had surrounded her seemed to dissipate, only to be replaced by a hollow sadness. All this joy was disappearing before her eyes. Dawson was getting married; Em leaving for High Honor. These moments, with all of them here to laugh together, would be gone except for Holiday once a year. No more days like this. No more moments like this.

A year from now, it would be just Mirren, alone with her mom making the salad while her dad set the table.

No Emory running around, bouncing off the walls and singing random songs that made them laugh. No Dawson to mess with her. Just Mirren. Alone.

Mirren looked down at the salad, suddenly feeling anything but joyful. How many more times would Mirren make dinner for them all? Dawson could propose any day now. They all knew it was coming. There was nothing to say Dawson wasn't planning on pulling them aside tonight to tell them he was planning to propose tomorrow. It would totally be like Dawson to tell them this last minute.

Tomorrow. It could be tomorrow. That would put their wedding in June. Right after Testing. Emory left in September. In six months, Mirren would be alone.

She'd always known this was coming. Plenty of people dealt with this—anyone with an older sibling. Why was it such a big deal to her?

She washed her hands slowly and dried them on a towel, then took the salad bowl from her mom and carried it to the table before sliding into her seat.

Why did this bother her so much? She didn't like feeling this way.

Emory fell into the seat next to her and accidentally knocked into her. She adjusted herself and grinned apologetically. "Sorry."

Mirren looked at her for a long moment—Emory's long blonde hair just like her own, her eyes full of life, always looking for something new to explore. She looked up and caught Mirren's eye, gave her a questioning look. Mirren shook her head and dropped her gaze back on her own place setting.

She was always annoyed with Emory growing up—they'd never been super close—but now the idea of her leaving made her feel nauseous.

Why was this bothering her? She'd always known it was coming.

Once dinner was cleaned up, Dawson headed upstairs, saying something about checking something in his room. A minute later, their father headed up, too, and then their mother. Mirren loaded their dishwasher with more force than necessary. Her fear had proven correct—Dawson was most definitely presenting his plan of proposal to her parents right now.

She wanted so badly to be happy for them; she loved Ashlyn, and they really were such a perfect match. Why, then, did it leave her feeling so upset inside?

Her gaze wandered over to Ashlyn, enthralled in a conversation with Emory, both of them animated and smiling as they talked.

Maybe it wouldn't be so bad. Like Saige had told her a million times over, it wasn't like she'd never see Dawson again. Maybe not as regularly, but he wasn't gone for good. And Mirren was gaining a sister, too. She'd never really thought of it that way. And soon maybe she'd have little nieces and nephews to dote on. That would be fun.

Maybe she was taking this too seriously.

Dawson had decided on the following Saturday to propose to Ashlyn. They'd both be over for dinner, as usual. They would set dinner out, but right before they started eating, he'd propose. It was exciting and terrifying all at once—that it was actually happening. Not that she'd ever doubted it would, but it just felt so weird that it was.

When she walked in the door from school, she felt the atmosphere of hushed secrecy and the excitement in the air, and silently began drilling herself with the reminders she had been all day: *it's okay to be excited. At least act like you are. Don't spoil their big moment.*

For all her attempts at convincing herself, it still felt like she was losing Dawson today.

Mirren stood in the foyer, shivering in her sweater. Why couldn't she just get excited for her siblings like normal people?

"Mom! Mirren's home!" Emory swept by, blonde

hair flying behind her. "Mirren, we need your help in the kitchen with the dessert." She spun on her heel and squealed. "I can't believe this is happening!"

"I—I can't, either." Mirren wrapped her arms around herself, trying to work up an excitement. All she could see were the losses.

"You okay, little sis?" Emory paused to look at her. "You can't be upset on your brother's biggest day!"

Mirren officially felt like the worst sister on the planet. She wished she could turn around and go back to find Risa and Saige. More accurately, Saige. Risa—that was another topic she didn't like thinking about anymore. But Saige—Saige was kind, and genuine, and funny, and seemed like the type of person that if Mirren showed up for dinner without calling ahead, she'd just hand her a plate of food without missing a beat.

Not that Risa wasn't like that—she'd just give Mirren a harder time for it. "Always accommodating Mirren," she'd joke, or, "Yeah, come on, Mirren, always interrupting our family dinners." She'd always smile as she said so, and Mirren knew she intended to joke, but her jokes weren't all that funny anymore and ended up wearing Mirren out more than she liked to let on.

Saige wasn't like that. Saige didn't say things she didn't mean.

"Ashlyn Foster..." Dawson bent on one knee, and Mirren's breath caught, and for a second she found it—that joy she wished she had for her brother. She looked at Ashlyn's glowing complexion, all her attention focused around the boy she loved kneeling in front of her. "Will you accept my offer to be your husband?"

Mirren watched Ashlyn's large eyes filled with tears of joy and she blinked them back before clasping her hands in front of her and spilling out, "I accept with all the joy within me!"

Of course Dawson and Ashlyn would be able to make the traditional lines personal and meaningful, and Mirren smiled. But then again, it wasn't like she'd been privy to many proposals in her life. She could recall being present when her cousin Emmett proposed to her now cousin-in-law Alia, but besides that, she didn't remember any others. Guilt bit at her. She had been young when her cousin's engagement happened, but she remembered being unable to stop grinning, so full of joy. She hadn't even been close with Emmett; how could she have been more happier for him than she was right now for her own brother?

But she was happy for Dawson—she was smiling now, and it grew as she watched the happy couple embrace. Emory was clapping giddily and her parents were close to tears. If anyone were watching, they'd think Mirren was loathsome to the whole situation due to the lack of excitement she was currently expressing.

What was wrong with her?

"Mirren!" Emory, oblivious to her sister's inner turmoil, spun her out of her chair. "We're going to have another sister!"

It took Mirren a moment to realize she meant Ashlyn, and that brought a genuine smile out of her. She really did like Ashlyn.

Her parents cheered, teary eyed, and exchanged looks of satisfaction, that they'd at least brought this child up right. They had a right to feel proud. Mirren remembered a friend of the family's a few years ago, whose daughter had missed her engagement season. Rumor had it she was still alone. Such a thing was scandalous.

It wasn't a criminal thing to have wished Dawson's engagement didn't have had to happen, was it? That was practically wishing her brother had defied standards. Mirren lowered her head, played with the fringe on her napkin, trying to gather the energy to at least act excited, for their sake. Maybe she was just tired. She didn't like the swimmy feeling in her mind, nor the strange thoughts intruding her mind.

Was she really so selfish and self-centered that she could only think of herself at a time like this?

"Ooooh, Ashlyn!" said Emory, who was still in the clouds. "I'm going to have so much fun planning the wedding with you!"

Ashlyn took a moment to jump up and down with Emory in excitement. "Obviously, because I've already decided you're going to be my wedding planner!"

"Me?" squealed Emory. "I'm not even out of high school yet!"

"You will be by the wedding!" said Ashlyn. "That's good enough for me! Besides, don't you want to go into a career of planning and organizing?"

"Yes! I want to be a Community Event Planner! Oooh, Ashlyn, you are absolutely the best!" Emory hugged Ashlyn tightly, excitement shining in her eyes, but then she broke away. "Everyone! I completely forgot! I in no ways intend to intercept Dawson and Ashlyn's moment, but I have an announcement of my own. I've decided to attend Westview for High Honor!"

That was so like Emory—no dramatic announcement when she was excited—it just spilled out of her. It took Mirren a minute to comprehend what she had heard.

Westview? But this wasn't a surprise. Emory had never been shy about the fact she wanted to go. But now that it was actually happening—

Mirren stared at her sister. "Em," she said. "Westview?"

"I know it's not in this community," Emory gushed, "but it's one of the top schools in the country, and I got accepted! And they specialize in social jobs— organizing and planning included! And of course it's highly recommended to go another community for experience when specializing in things that have to do with community! It's everything I ever could have wanted. And Eden is going, too! What are the chances my dream school could include my best friend?" Emory collapsed in a chair, finally having exhausted her excitement, sighing happily. "Life keeps getting better and better!"

While the rest of the family cheered and gushed and congratulated Em, Mirren couldn't stop thinking about how her life was just getting worse and worse.

Testing, as always, brought even more unwelcome anxiety upon her.

She was used to it; ever since her low score in First Level, Testing had always been something she dreaded throughout the year. She usually tried to channel that fear into positive energy, studying extra hard and putting her all into it—and she supposed it had worked, so far.

But how long could she keep it up if it had really been a façade this whole time? If she was meant to have been withdrawn in first level?

Mirren, stop. Deep breath in, deep breath out. She was always emotional this time of year; and this year, it was simply amplified because of everything going on with Dawson and Emory. She'd get through—she'd be fine. Just because Emory and Dawson were both leaving didn't mean they didn't love her less. It just meant it didn't faze them to leave her.

The morning of Testing, her parents were already up when she got downstairs and her mom came over to give her a hug. "No matter what, I'm proud of you, sweetie," she said, like she did every year, but for some reason all Mirren heard was the asterisk next to her words: for if she received orange—she couldn't even let herself imagine red—there was no parent in the world who would be proud of her. Orange was disgraceful.

She just wouldn't score orange. Simple.

She really did love her family and her friends.

But it was becoming harder to believe that they truly loved her, and she didn't know where that fear came from.

⸱⸱⸱⸱⸱•••••••••••••••••••••••••••••••••••⸱⸱⸱⸱⸱

Sitting in the chair in the Testing room, staring down at the Test, the bold words blurring together, she suddenly felt a wave of anxiety like she never had before descend upon her.

Would anybody care if she scored too low?

Would anything change about anyone's lives?

QUESTION #2. What was the central theme of this story?

Dawson would still get married, if she were withdrawn. Emory would still go to school. Her parents would start getting ready for life as grandparents, once Dawson had kids, which would probably be not long after he got married. Saige—Saige seemed to care, but even her life would go on. Risa—she didn't want to think about Risa.

Risa hadn't been the one standing with her when her score was announced. Risa wasn't the one coming over to check up on her. Her friend had practically disappeared off the face of the earth, or, if she saw her, only muttering pleasantries. Was she ashamed of Mirren? Was she embarrassed to be her friend?

QUESTION #3. Who was the main character, and what was her best trait?

But she couldn't think of any of this now—she had the Test—

The Test!

QUESTION #4. If this story took place in our world, what would be different?

She looked back down at the page—she had answered one question—only one?

Panic. She flipped the page, then flipped back. Her future rested on this. A future that potentially affected nobody.

Her breath came in gasps.

This was only the school portion of the Test—

testing her education. If she couldn't even get past this—
the presumably easy portion—

But she *knew* how to analyze a story!

Why was she letting this get to her? She had been so
good at keeping it in check before.

**QUESTION #5. What character flaws did the main character
demonstrate?**

She tried to imagine what her parents would say when they
found her afterwards. Probably, "We can't wait to see your
amazingly high scores!"

Such faith they had in her. She feared it was mis-
placed.

When her score came back, it felt like her whole life crashed
down around her. She had dared believe that first level
screw-up had been a one-time mistake; from the words of
her family and friends she had dared believe she could overcome that, could be more than that—but it had all been
lies.

Lies maybe they even said to themselves. But that
would imply they cared about her. Mirren couldn't get the
image of her parents' horrified faces out of her mind when

the announcer read off her score. Almost like her parents had expected her to warn them somehow. How was she supposed to know? And nothing on the Test had been directly difficult—only her panic that had prevented her from scoring the best she could—right?

She felt like she couldn't even understand herself anymore, and it made her miserable, like she was lost in a maze with no way out, like no matter how fast she ran, no matter how hard she tried, she kept hitting dead ends.

The Monday after scores were revealed, she found her new schedule tacked up over her usual one, and it made her stomach sink into nausea.

She clenched her fists, fighting the descending hopelessness. She only had three months of this; if she put her all into it, looked on the positive side—she could get through it. She knew she could. But as she stared at the schedule, she felt her determination sink lower and lower. To what avail? What if she poured everything into this and still got withdrawn at the end?

Was it even worth it to try anymore?

Saige would grab her by the shoulders, shake her, tell her yes, of course it was!

She closed her eyes, breathed in deeply.

She could at least try. For Saige. For more than Saige, but for now, Saige was going to be her key motivation.

She twisted her hair into a topknot and tried to pretend she didn't already know that that was the hairstyle designated for girls who scored as low as she did. A way to set apart from society those who might soon leave. To warn those around her that she could be dangerous.

She wasn't going to leave, though. She wasn't.

Her clothing was different for the same reason—so people around would know she was a lower class member in society. So they could steer clear of her. She thought of what Saige would do, and figured Saige would probably make the best of it, so she stared down at her outfit, at the orange shirt with its high neck and small sleeves, at the faded denim shorts. Faded, because they were the ones who didn't get processed as well. Nothing but the best for imperfects, Mirren thought sarcastically as she laced up her shoes—at least those were still her normal ones—and took a step back to look at herself fully in the mirror.

She bit her lip down so hard she drew blood. Of course it was intentional that every part of her screamed, "I'm an Orange student!"

Three months, she said to herself weakly. *Three months.*

And in three months, Emory would be leaving for High Honor.

What a fantastic way to spend her last few months with her sister. Emory was already avoiding her any chance she got, and Mirren didn't blame her.

Nobody wanted to be seen with imperfections.

Saige wouldn't mind. Mirren redid her hair, checking the time carefully. Her schedule allowed her a few free hours on Saturday. She could go see Saige. That could be her motivation. Saige wouldn't give her a hard time about it. Saige would probably have forgotten it even happened. Saige was just like that.

She followed the directions on the schedule and arrived at the building where they held the orange classes right on time and found the room quickly. She slipped in silently and found the desk with her name on it toward the back.

Toward the back because she was the most hopeless?

She didn't know anyone else in the class; there was only one other girl in high school, and the rest were younger levels. Uneasiness crept upon her; she felt sick; she didn't belong here.

Breathe in, breathe out. At the end of the week she could see Saige.

But right now all she could see were the long hours that she had to get through before that.

She felt like she couldn't breathe. Her heart raced. Was this what a panic attack felt like? She gripped the edges of her desk, closed her eyes, and tried to steady her rapidly beating heart. *It's okay. I'm okay.*

But she had never felt less okay in her life.

. . . .

"Before we begin, let's go over the basic rules." Orange teachers were known for their coldness and strictness. Mirren had grown up being taught this was essential. That there was no wiggle room for orange students. Most people, her family, her friends, thought it a good standard. Mirren never did. Probably because of her personal experience. She shifted uneasily in her seat; was this the same room she'd come to in first level, or had they switched locations since then? This was bringing back too many unwanted memories.

So much of that year—her first level year—still remained seared in her mind. She raised her hand in response to the teacher's statement on rules, and the teacher surprised her by calling on her. "No talking unless called on. Attention must be rapt on instructor at all times. Direct focus is required. No leaving the classroom unless for a bathroom or drink break. No outside sources." She flawlessly recited the rules, and then immediately wanted to shrink into a ball and hide. What was she thinking? Now she was the weird one to all of them, too—they would know she had been here before.

She wanted to cry. She had practically sealed her own fate. No special attention would be given to her, now that they knew she was a returner. A horrifying thought sent chills down her spine—what even were her odds? She never heard of people going through the orange program more than once.

What if this was a joke? What if they had only told her she could attend classes as a cruel prank, when all along they had planned to just withdraw her? Wasn't that the penalty for multiple orange scores anyway? Or had they extended her another grace period out of pity? What kind of existence would that be—to constantly be granted exactly what she needed because people pitied her? Could she ever be more than this? She fought for her breath, tried to pay attention to the teacher, tried to act like she was present in the room when really she had never felt more far away.

What was happening to her?

When she got home, nobody greeted her. She walked into the kitchen, sat down at the counter, expecting, hoping, her mother to at least ask about her day. But all her mother said was, "Come help me with the spaghetti, please, Mirren."

Emory got home and there was no reaction from her, either. She hardly acknowledged Mirren as she got herself a cup of water before launching into an excited narrative of her day, to which her mother responded favorably.

Were they ignoring her because they were ashamed?

Because they didn't believe she'd score high enough and figured it'd be an easier departure if they stopped paying attention to her now?

Mirren wasn't sure which she preferred.

It was becoming harder and harder to follow through on the optimism she was determined to hold this morning.

* * *

The next day was even harder than the first. She trekked her way to class and had trouble getting in the building.

But if she didn't go—if she didn't go, her fear would be her reality.

But what if it was anyway?

She took a breath, then she walked in, sat down. Her classmates regarded her warily, like she was worse off than them. It was probably true.

She tried her best to pay attention throughout the day's lesson—they were starting off with school subjects, today math—but it all was easy and simple, too simple for her, though obviously it wasn't if she had scored so low.

She waited anxiously all day to just leave and go

home, but when she finally stepped through the door of her house at dinnertime, she wanted nothing more than to go somewhere else, somewhere where people at least pretended to care about her and didn't act like she had ceased to exist.

On her way to and from Orange classes, people kept their distance, some giving her scornful looks, others not even looking her direction.

Maybe she was truly a harm to her world, and she just couldn't see it.

risa | PART 4

SUMMER SCHEDULES - HIGH SCHOOL LEVEL STUDENT #234 -
RISA COLETTE DOBBIN

8:00 Rise
          Get out of bed/extra time   (3 minutes)
          Get dressed   (3 minutes)
          Make bed   (5 minutes)
          Brush teeth & wash face   (4 minutes)
          Hairstyle   (5 minutes)
8:20 Breakfast
8:40 Cleanup
9:00 Study
10:00 Recreation
12:00 Lunch
1:00 Cleanup
1:15 Outdoor
2:30 Social
4:00 Outing
5:30 Relax
6:00 Dinner
6:30 Cleanup
7:00 Social
9:30 Shower
10:00 Prepare for Bed
          Pajamas on   (3 minutes)
          Brush teeth/wash face   (4 minutes)
          Clean room   (7 minutes)
          Hairstyle   (5 minutes)
10:30 Quiet Time
11:00 Lights Out

When Risa first learned of Mirren's score, she blatantly disregarded it. Not Mirren, perfect-scoring, brilliant Mirren? The same Mirren who never got below Blue in her entire life? How did something like this possibly happen? If she hadn't known better, Risa might have even said there had been a mistake made; but of course in this community there were no such mistakes made.

Risa made up her mind, the day she found out, that she was going to do everything she could to be the friend Mirren needed. This was when her friend would need her most.

But the first day she went to find Mirren, Mirren wasn't home, and Risa couldn't find her anywhere.

She went to bed that night anxious, worried she had missed something, worried about Mirren. Should she have looked longer for her today? But it was good Mirren hadn't been home—it meant she had found something to do. Maybe she had gone with Emory or Dawson somewhere.

The next morning, she slid into a seat at the counter next to Brynlee, her eight-year-old sister, who immediately began chattering about her day and her plans as Risa fixed them both breakfast. "Can you check your tracker for me, Brynlee?" she gently interrupted her sister, and Brynlee nodded, jumping up from her seat and her dark hair swinging behind her as she went over to her nutrient tracker on the side of the fridge. Brynlee's tracker was slightly different from the typical one Risa and her parents followed because of her differing health needs.

Risa watched her trace her finger along the foods for today and then spin around to the fridge. "I get toast with bananas today!" she said. "You guys get boring eggs, but I get toast and bananas." She emphasized her words happily as she set about making her meal. Risa watched her for a moment, and then set to work.

From an early age they had realized that certain foods made Brynlee sick, something rare in their community of perfection and schedules. They had taken her to several doctors, even some outside their community, and there had been a scary time when they were worried Brynlee would get withdrawn because of contagion—but then the medical records had come through, and she wasn't dangerous, just inconvenient, and so finally they'd come up with the solution to just give her an altered diet that excluded those foods that made her sick. The diet didn't always work, and they'd had several scares over the years, but they'd all been diffused, so far anyway. This was just the life they had, and they had learned to deal with it.

"Risa, guess what? Today I'm going with Savannah to the movie theater to see *Escape the Cape*. And after that we're going to go the bakery, and I know I'm technically not supposed to go there because last time I got sick, but Savannah went there a few weeks ago and said she found something there with no eggs, or milk, and so it'd be safe for me to have! So—"

"That's great, Brynlee," Risa said, irritated and not in the mood to listen to her sister's endless chatter. "Tell me all about it later, okay?" She softened her tone, and Brynlee shrugged. "Okay!"

After study hour, she slipped on her shoes and set out to find Mirren, determined today. The short walk to her friend's house felt nice; the warm air seemed to promise a good day ahead.

When she reached Mirren's house, her friend was just coming outside, but when she saw Risa, her face went tense. "Hey."

"Hey, stranger." Risa tried to ignore the obvious

tension in her friend's voice. Mirren was under a lot of stress right now. "How you doing?"

"Fine." Mirren walked down the steps toward her. "You?"

"Good. Hey, I went looking for you Saturday, but—"

"I was with Saige."

"Ah. Well…you want to hang out? Go somewhere?"

Mirren shrugged, biting her fingernail as she walked. "Whatever you want is fine." She was never this dismissive, disregarding. Risa caught up to her, walking backwards so she could look at her. What was her deal? Had Risa done something? "Hey, is something up? You mad at me for anything?"

Mirren regarded her warily. "Why would I be mad at you?" she said.

Risa didn't reply. "Want to go find Saige?"

Mirren shook her head. "She's busy today."

They walked a bit, in silence, then suddenly Risa spun around, right in front of her life so Mirren had to stop, too. Mirren's face mirrored Risa's frustration. "What do you want now, Risa?"

The words stung. Risa bit back the hurt growing within her, and she knew she should restrain it, hold it back. Except she didn't. "What on earth is your deal, Mirren? I've been your biggest supporter all the way through, and this is how you treat me?"

"*You*?" Mirren said, her voice quiet but piercing. "*You* weren't there when I got my score. You haven't been over all week."

Risa turned her words over. "Mirren, I don't have orange schedules memorized!" she cried. "I just figured you'd come find me, you know, since we're best friends and all." The bitterness in her words bit at the air around them.

She hoped Mirren felt it. Her friend had no right to treat her this way, no matter what she went through. "So, let me guess, you and your real best friend Saige have been having special moments together every weekend?" Of course they were. "And neither of you ever thought of me? Is that all I am to you?"

Mirren didn't react.

"Some people are actually friends to me, Risa." Mirren spoke without emotion, but her words pierced all the same. Her expression had collapsed. Without another word, she turned and walked away.

Risa watched her go, had the longing to run after her, apologize, beg her friend to talk to her. But instead she clenched her fists and turned to walk away.

When she got home, the house was quiet, but that wasn't abnormal—social hour hadn't ended yet, after all, and her parents and Brynlee would be out with friends. Risa slipped her shoes off, shoved them into their spot on the rack, and walked into the kitchen. "Anybody here?" Sometimes Brynlee brought friends home, but there was no response.

Risa heaved a sigh and filled a glass with water from the sink. She took a long drink, staring out the back window, her thoughts a blur. She could sense the anger piling up within her, and she didn't know how to manage it. Didn't want to manage it.

The front door slammed, and she jumped. "Hello?"

"Risa?" Her father appeared in the threshold to the kitchen, and Risa went cold at the tremor in his voice and the fear on his face.

"Something's happened to Brynlee," was all he said.

The air outside seemed suddenly cold, even though it was in the middle of summer.

Her heartbeat thudded, echoing in her ears, drowning out other noises as they walked. "What happened?"

Her father's pale expression etched itself in her mind. But surely everything was fine. Brynlee had had scares before. She'd always been fine.

"I'm not sure, Risa." His voice was low, his gaze direct ahead of them. "It doesn't look good."

Risa blinked rapidly. "What is that supposed that

mean?"

He didn't answer, and she blinked faster. "But she'll be okay, right?"

There was no reply this time either, and suddenly Risa came alive and ran—she ran, faster and faster, to the only place Brynlee would be—the medical center. Her heart throbbed in her chest as she left the quiet neighborhood streets and turned down the streets of the busy downtown, dodging people as she went. Her legs ached, but she couldn't stop. Her father was at her heels. When she finally reached the building and burst through the doors, her mother was there, her expression overrun by agony and she swept Risa up in her arms. Her sobs shook Risa to her core, and she pushed her mother away roughly. "Where's my sister?"

Risa didn't wait for an answer. She pushed past her mother and ran back toward the hallways, pushing away medical personnel until she realized she didn't know where Brynlee was; even then she ran, opening and closing doors, her heart racing, her eyes wild, completely unfamiliar with this painful emotion coursing through her—

"Brynlee!" A breathless cry. Her sister: motionless on one of the beds, her dark hair still braided from this morning, her eyes closed. Wires, weird machinery, buzzing machines attached to her sweet sister. Risa couldn't breathe, and she turned to face back the way she had come, bracing herself in the doorway. Just focus on breathing. In and out. In and out. Surely this kind of thing happened often. She knew it was a falsity even before the thought finished running through her mind. These kind of things never happened. Those who were this sick were always withdrawn early on.

What had even happened? What was even wrong?

Risa turned and walked, slowly, slowly, toward Brynlee. Her sister's small form rose and fell with steady breathing, and relief melted over Risa with an intensity that nearly knocked her over. She crouched down at the bedside, steadying herself by synchronizing her breathing with her sister's. But panic only continued to rise, for with a calm mind came the crashing reality—for Brynlee to be here, there were only three possible outcomes.

She could make a full recovery.

She could die.

Or she would be withdrawn.

Her sister had already been walking the fine line of being healthy enough versus too sick her entire life. Something like this...

She became aware of other people behind her and turned to see her parents. She met their eyes, her own wild with desperation. "Please tell me what's going on."

"We're—we're not sure." Risa's mother collapsed to her knees next to her daughter, her eyes only on Brynlee.

"She was fine this morning...this afternoon...you saw her, you know. She went to the bakery with Savannah for social...you know what happened the last time she went there. I don't know why she thought it was okay to go again. I was told her face swelled up within seconds and she started gasping for breath—they brought her here—she's been like...like this ever since." He swallowed and pressed a hand to his face, unable to say more.

Risa, too, swallowed hard, the reality of what this meant crashing down upon her. Brynlee was no longer stable.

Which meant—

If she—

—If she survived, she wasn't compatible with their society anymore.

They would withdraw her.

Either way, she was losing her sister. Forever.

Her worries and fears about her friendships and drama now seemed trivial. She stared at her sister, expressionless, feeling the gravity of the situation consuming her, of how suddenly, suddenly, somehow, her life had taken a dark turn she could have never expected.

They still gave her a ceremony.

As if she was old, having lived a long life, and now had peacefully passed on.

Not like she had been a sprightly eight year old with an excitement for what lay in her future, a future she'd now never get.

Risa hadn't even been able to say goodbye.

Dark days and nights turned into dark weeks.

Risa hid in her room, taking the full advantage of grieving schedules, never speaking to anyone and making up reasons to avoid parts of the schedule intended to "help" her—such as "talk to a friend," or, "go for a walk."

Withdrawal was something she was familiar with, as painful as it was. This wasn't withdrawal. This was more final than withdrawal. This was death, something foreign and unknown, and it scared her, encompassed her, crushed her.

How had she let this take her so by surprise? Surely she had known, in the back of her mind, that this could have happened at any time. Except she hadn't. She hadn't even though it a distant possibility.

How could she go to school this year without making the stop to drop Brynlee off at her bus stop? How could she come home with no happy girl to say, "Risa, guess what

I learned today?"

Nobody to make her smile; nobody to brag on; no-body to annoy her.

Her friends didn't come around. Saige had been kind in the beginning, but after a few times of being re-jected when stopping by, she'd stopped coming. And who knew what Mirren's deal was—she hadn't shown her face once since it happened. And Risa's parents—they were too far distanced in their own grief.

The day it happened, she had told Brynlee to be quiet. Leave her alone. If she'd only known. She could have told Brynlee not to go to the bakery. She could have changed this. She remembered Brynlee mentioning it to her. Everything might have been different, if she had only paid attention a little more.

She dreamed of her sister, and woke in the middle of the night, tears wet on her cheeks, and heard them again. Footsteps. Outside her window.

What did she have left to lose? She carefully, qui-etly, quickly, climbed out of bed, to the window, and looked out. Her breath caught, and she felt like her heart stopped: a group of kids, girls, it looked like, probably her age, tiptoeing down the neighborhood streets, barely visible in the darkness of night.

What on earth were they doing?

She sat at the window for a minute, eyes narrowed,

watching them until they left her line of view. Who were they, and what exactly did they think they were doing? If they were caught, they'd be withdrawn for sure.

Should she tell someone about this?

As quickly as the thought entered it left. Why should she care? It didn't matter. But was that how she was going to live her life from now on? Just not caring about anything because it wasn't worth it? Was this going to be the end of Risa's life, too? This was it? Just one thing happened and she gave up all will to really live?

She grunted and made her way back to bed. She didn't want to live like this. But at the same time, she knew she wouldn't forget about Brynlee, no matter how hard she tried.

The next day when she woke up, her regular schedule was framed in the place it had always been, the place where it had been replaced by grieving schedules.

Had it really been two weeks?

Her face crumpled. She hated the schedule, longed to slam her fist against it and watch the glass in the frame shatter to the ground.

But she knew better.

Did she? It wasn't like she was going to follow the thing anyway.

What would she do next week, then? Just skip school? Ruin her own life? What would that do to her parents? Well, then again, it wasn't like they were doing just fine right now anyway.

It was like a war within Risa, an angry debate in her own mind, and she didn't even know which side was right anymore.

She knew her schedule like the back of her hand, so she didn't even bother checking it, only glanced at the clock every so often. Maybe the familiar habits would help. The standards that framed her life could help get her through. If she wanted to be helped, which she wasn't sure she did.

Her mom was in the kitchen making breakfast. Risa stopped in the doorway and crossed her arms. "So this is it?"

"Excuse me?"

"Grieving schedules end, and bam! Back to everyday life. Pretend she never existed." Risa hated the tone in her words and did nothing to stop it.

"Risa," said her mother, but her voice faltered, and she said nothing else.

Risa spun on her heel. "I'll be back later. I don't need breakfast. Bye."

When she got to the bus stop, nobody said anything, but she could see their questioning gazes as they stared at her out of the corner of their eyes, like they thought she couldn't see them that way.

She grunted "Good morning" at them, but, unsurprisingly, received no response. The buses pulled up, and as she was boarding, it occurred to her for the first time that since she had missed beginning-of-the-year orientation, she had no idea what her schedule was.

She'd have to go to the office when she got there, and that meant she'd be late for classes and not have time to get her books from her locker. How much worse could this day get?

She found her seat—number 36—one thing that was thankfully the same as last year. She dropped her bag on the hook attached to the seat in front of her, pulled the seat belt over her lap, and then turned to face the window, unwilling to talk to anyone.

"Risa?" She ignored the voice, though her heart panged with recognition, and she clenched her teeth as her best friend—if she could still be called that—slid into the seat next to her.

If Risa had been more alert, she might have noticed the way the kids spread away from Mirren like the plague when she walked by, or the way the kid across the aisle—the next closest to her—scooted as far away from her as he could get.

"I got your schedule for you at orientation," Mirren said, and a piece of paper floated into Risa's lap. Absently she picked it up, wanting to feel grateful and hopeful but only feeling the frustration inside of her. Now she'd be obligated to talk, and she really didn't feel like speaking even a word.

"Fine," Mirren said. "Be that way." She clicked her own buckle and didn't say anything more. Finally. Risa didn't make any move to change the silence between them.

A part of her itched to say she was sorry; to hug her friend and let Mirren comfort her. But whether it was her pride, her anger, or even the weird feeling that something wasn't quite right about her friend anymore, something in her made her stay as far away as possible.

When they got off the bus, Mirren didn't wait for her at the bottom. Risa knew she had brought it upon herself, but it still stung. At least now she'd be on time and not have to go through all the logistical problems. She took in a deep breath of fall air as she walked. Maybe she could let go of this and move on.

She watched Mirren walk in ahead of her and thought back to days of their tight-knit friendship. She still wasn't sure when things had changed, or how.

The school day was longer than she remembered, and more draining, too. People were polite to her, but she felt the unspoken pity behind every word. She wished they'd stop.

Saige found her at lunch period and hugged her long and tight. "How are you feeling?"

Risa still didn't understand Saige's desire to pour into her all of a sudden. "I'm fine," she said tightly, pulling away and sitting down at the table. Saige, of course, sat down next to her. What was it with Saige? Who did she think she was, that she somehow knew Risa's pain better than everyone else?

"What is your deal, Saige?" Risa said through gritted teeth, already regretting her words. "You act like you're so—I don't know—so—so above everyone else, like you know exactly what I'm going through, but how can I trust you? What, let me guess, you lost a sister just Brynlee's age too?"

She saw the shock from her tone register on Saige's face and she wished she could take her words back. But before she could say anything, Saige spoke, her eyes piercing Risa's.

"Her name was Cassie," she said.

⋅ ⋅ ⋅ ⋅ ⋅ ⋅ ⋅ • ⋅ ⋅ ⋅ ⋅ ⋅ ⋅

Risa slammed her locker with more force than necessary. She didn't want to deal with guilt now.

Who did Saige think she was, trying to fix all of Risa's problems? Had she truly lost a sister too? Why had

Risa never heard of Cassie before? Wouldn't she have heard someone talk about it? Yet—she had heard the tone in Saige's voice, and she recognized it from hearing it in her own, and in her heart she knew Saige was telling the truth.

But that was too hard to dwell upon: too hard to believe that Saige really did know, because how Risa had treated her was something she was not proud of. And she didn't have the slightest idea how to fix it. Any of it. Her life was falling apart at the seams and she could do nothing to fix any of it.

PART 5

Saige found Archer in his room during relax hour one night, laying on his bed and reading a book. She lingered in the doorway, leaned up against the doorframe, studying him.

He looked up from his book, saw her, and put the book down. "Saige?"

"Did you hear about the Dobbins' little girl who got sick and withdrawn?" Saige blurted, dropping onto the bed. "The one who was on her deathbed?"

"I did," said Archer, slowly, then he eyed her carefully. "That's Risa's sister, isn't it?"

She nodded.

Archer shook his head. "That's awful. Is she doing okay? Risa?"

"I don't know." Did he not see the correlation to their own lives? Was he really missing the hints she was trying to drop? "Losing a sister is really hard. She probably isn't doing that great."

Now he was staring at her.

"She's ten years old now," Saige whispered.

He returned her fiery, heartbroken gaze, neither of them knowing what to say.

"Ten years old," he repeated.

Saige nodded wordlessly, swallowing hard.

"Ten," he said again.

"Ten," Saige said.

"How old was Brynlee?" he asked her.

"Seven, I think," she said, swallowing again. "Have you talked to Risa?"

"Briefly.... She won't talk to anyone, Archer."

He looked away. "You were the same way. She'll be okay."

Saige looked away, too. "But what if I never was okay?" she said, her voice small, but penetrating the air around them. "What if it was only an act I learned to play extremely well? What if I still have nightmares about saying goodbye to her at night? What if her memory still haunts me?" She stared down at her hands, dreading his answer, hating herself for being so vulnerable but also knowing she didn't regret what she'd said.

Archer was silent for a long time. "Then you'd be just like me," he finally said.

She figured Mirren would be home during social hour the next day, but her house stood quiet and empty. Lingering on the sidewalk, she was surprised by the disappointment that welled up within her—as well as some confusion. This morning at school Mirren had said she'd be home today, and it wasn't like she had a lot of people talking to her right now.

Her attitude souring, she was reminded of the distance growing between her and Mirren, ever since Dawson's wedding.

What had she done wrong?

Unless—Risa. That was where Mirren could be, though last Saige knew, the two weren't talking. Saige turned to go, ignoring the bitterness tempting to descend. Where else would Mirren be?

But if Risa was spending time with a friend, it was good. For both of them, actually. It was good. Good. Saige held onto that with all her might as she walked slowly back home, the threat of an empty schedule for the first time not even entering her mind.

Risa didn't know what compelled her to walk the all-too-familiar path to Mirren's house, land a knock on the door, and stand on the doorstep until her friend opened the door and met her with a stony gaze.

"I don't want to talk to you, Risa," Mirren said through her teeth.

"Mirren—I know you don't. Just give me a minute." Deep breath in, deep breath out. But trying to calm down was a fruitless attempt with the fiery gaze still covering Mirren's features, and instead, an intense sadness fell upon her. What happened to the Mirren she knew? The Mirren who would have come over the moment she heard of Brynlee even if it meant just sitting there and doing nothing?

Risa had just lived through her worst nightmare, and what had Mirren done? Just kept on living in her own little bubble, throwing herself pity parties.

"What do you want?" Mirren said, leaning on the doorjam and holding the door barely open.

Don't get angry, don't get angry. Mirren has had her own share of troubles.

What? Had she lost a sister?

Anger fizzled within her. "Where have you been, Mirren?" The words were out of her mouth before she could think, and before she could take them back, Mirren was yelling. At her. "Where have I been? Oh, you mean like, where was I when Brynlee was withdrawn?" Her face twisted, and she pulled back from the door. "You think the entire world revolves around you, huh? Well, maybe you're not the only one with problems!"

Risa's watch dinged, but she ignored it, her feet glued to the ground, a sour taste filling her mouth. "Oh, so now I'm not allowed to have any problems, am I? I'm just supposed to maintain the role as your perfect best friend no matter what?" she shot back before she could think.

"Perfect? No." Every word Mirren spoke was over-exaggerated and sarcastic. "My friend? Yes. You ask me where I've been? Where were *you* when I was struggling through my Orange classes? My own family won't talk to me! And even though my best friend—*you*—promised me she'd always be there for me, she ditched me, too! You wonder why I didn't talk to you all summer? Maybe because it's because you never talked to me."

The words hit their mark, and Risa stepped backward. An apology hovered on her tongue, but Mirren was talking again, her expression frustrated as she roughly spoke in such an un-Mirren-like manner that it scared Risa. "You have no idea what I've been through, Risa. But do you care? No, you do not. You only care about yourself and your pithy problems!"

Her face paled when the words left her lips, and for a second Risa thought she might try to take them back—

but her face only hardened as she crossed her arms tightly.

Any apology Risa had been considering evaporated. "Pithy? My sister gets taken away from me, forever, and you call that pithy?" she replied, her voice eerily controlled.

"Listen, I'm sorry if Emory doesn't talk to you, but at least you have a sister."

"Listen," Mirren shot back, her face twisting more with every word, her expression reddening. "I'm sorry about Brynlee. But at least with her, you can say it wasn't really her fault. Or your fault. It was an error, right, isn't that what they're saying?

"When I get withdrawn, Risa, do you know what everybody's going to say? They're going to say, 'She's had that coming a long time.' They're going to say, 'Well, we all saw that coming.' They're going to say, 'At least they finally got her out of here.' I am worth nothing to this world, nothing to my family, nothing even to you, and now you want to just prance up to me and expect me to be your best friend? Because that's all I am to you, isn't it, Risa? You didn't care about me when I was in the worst season of my life. You didn't care about me when I got handed pretty much the worst fate this world has to offer.

"But when your problems arise, oh, then you want to be my friend. I really don't care about your problems anymore, Risa. I don't care. I don't care about anybody or anything in this whole world. I really hope you can all do yourself a favor and just leave me alone!"

Tears streamed down her cheeks, and she heaved in heavy breaths, but her expression didn't change from its vicious stare. The sound of her labored breathing filled the space between them until without warning she turned and ran.

Risa wanted to yell after her.

She wanted to chase after her.

But instead of chasing her down, she too turned and walked away, her arms clutched tightly around herself, trying to put every word of their conversation out of her head.

"So, how are you doing?" Saige asked as they walked.

She had been excited to see Mirren when her friend showed up at her house, but her friend didn't seem to reflect her happiness.

"I told you, I'm fine," Mirren replied. "You?"

Something inside Saige told her something wasn't right, but she pushed it away. "I'm great."

"That's great," Mirren said without enthusiasm.

"Hey, where were you yesterday?" Saige tried. "I came over like we planned, but nobody was home."

Mirren shrugged this off. "I don't know why you do

that."

"Do what?"

"Come to see me and all. You win the award for the one and only." She said something under her breath and rolled her eyes, but there was a heaviness to her words. Saige stopped walking and looked at Mirren, who wouldn't return her gaze. "Hey—Mirren, we've talked about this. It's going to be okay. What's going on?"

Mirren spun around to face her, her expression worn. "Saige, you do know that since my score, nobody talks to me. Nobody checks in on me, or sees how I'm doing, not my parents, not my siblings—"

"I know," Saige interrupted. "We've talked about this."

"You don't have to do this, Saige!" Mirren exclaimed, sorrow painting her features. "It's not like..." She stopped, turning away.

"Like what?"

When Mirren turned back to face her, her face was worn, and her voice was dull as she spoke. "It's not like it's really going to matter. Like I matter at all to this world. Satisifed?"

"What?" Saige exclaimed. "That's ridiculous, Mirren! You may have been an orange student this summer, but you're not anymore!"

Mirren mumbled something under her breath.

"What?"

"Not like that matters. You think everything magically changed when the announcer said, 'Mirren Chase, Score of Green'?" She made air quotes, her voice sarcastic. "I hate to burst your bubble, but it didn't, Saige."

Saige hadn't known Mirren had passed by so little margin.

"What's going on?" she suddenly cried. "You're so tense and—not yourself. Where did my sweet friend go?" She fought to keep the desperation out of her voice.

Mirren didn't meet her eyes. "I think the orange classes killed her," she said, an edge to her voice.

Saige stood there a moment, the words sinking in, then she shook her head rapidly, words already tumbling out of her. "No. Mirren, your score doesn't define you. It never will define you. You can not let this take you down. You have to show the world! You aren't a worthless part of society. You aren't!"

There was no change in Mirren's expression. "Yeah? How about this. What if I am? 'Scores don't define me'? Ummm, they kinda do, Saige. If I score too low, I never see any of you again. If I score barely good enough, I get treated like some strange outcast, like everyone just wishes I'd be withdrawn already. If I score high, people throw me parties and recognize me as an honor student. How many times that happens determines what High Honor I go to, what job I get, and how much I'll contribute to this community! If I score too low, I don't matter anymore. I'd say my score matters!"

Saige couldn't believe the words coming from Mirren's mouth, but at the same time, chills raced up her spine at the bits of reality woven into her friend's words. "I never said your score didn't matter," she argued. "I said it doesn't define you. Your score might determine what you do in life, but it doesn't determine who you are."

Mirren's sour tone matched her expression. "Well, even you just said that I'm not myself anymore since scoring Orange. So maybe it does. Ever think about that?"

Saige shook her head again. "You know that's not true," she tried, but Mirren was having none of it. Her friend stepped back, her expression disgusted. "Why do you even care anyway?"

Saige was having trouble processing it all. "Because I'm your friend," she said, confused.

"Maybe I don't want you to be my friend," Mirren said vehemently, then she spun on her heel and walked away.

Saige opened her mouth to call after her, but nothing came out, and helplessness consumed her.

september, year 99 | **22**

School. It had already been three weeks into the school year, and wake-up call back at seven-ten was still taking some getting used to. Saige went through her routine, in disbelief that it was already this time of year again.

Tying the final loop in her elastic over her side braid, she glanced at the clock to find she had an extra minute, and took it to study herself in the mirror for a moment. Her brown hair looked limp in its thin braid; her hazel eyes were light; the freckle on her forehead was right where it'd always been. But that wasn't all there was to her—when people looked at her, did they see beyond her appearance, into who she was? And was she the Saige she wanted to be?

She'd thought she was finally doing okay, but after the fight with Mirren...She shook the thought away. Her friend was just going through a rough patch, but she'd get over it. She had to.

Downstairs, she ate her breakfast silently as Archer

prattled on about how excited he was for the first day of his last year of school. At seven-forty-five, they said goodbye to their parents, who were also getting ready to leave, and dashed out their corresponding bus stops: Archer at level thirteen, Saige at level eleven. She greeted the others who arrived, trying to be friendly and also divert her mind from thinking too much about Mirren. Risa, too. She hadn't seen her friend since before everything happened with her sister.

Thinking about it still twisted her on the inside.

At Mirren's stop, she resisted the urge to stare out the window and instead tried to catch Mirren's eye as her friend walked past, but Mirren ignored her completely. Oh well. Saige shifted, sighed, and looked back out the window. This was too much to keep track of.

By the time they rolled up to school, a strange, unidentifiable feeling had settled like a pit in Saige's stomach, and she couldn't figure out why.

The *rest* of rest hour was nonexistent, and dinner was silent.

During study period, Risa sat at her desk, tapping her fingers, staring at her wall, most definitely not studying, when there was a knock at the door, downstairs, and she froze.

In a past time, it might have been Mirren, coming over to study together, or one of Brynlee's friends.

Today, in a time where neither of those possibilities were possibilities, a knock couldn't be anything good.

She felt it creeping up her spine, and then down, forming a pit in her stomach.

"Risa?" Her father's voice—twisted and strange, like it had been when he had told her Brynlee was dying. She willed herself not to shake as she left her bedroom, crept down the stairs to see the law personnel waiting with a firm, determined look, and the fear skyrocketed.

She stood halfway down the staircase, gripping the railing, running possible scenarios through her mind, none of which she could get any logic to line up with.

"Miss Dobbin." The law official addressed her, and she looked weakly at her parents, standing behind him, holding each other. "I am here concerning the withdrawal order of Mirren Chase. I understand you know her?"

⬤ ⬤

Saige was reading in her room that night, after dinner and family hour, trying to distract her mind from all her sudden anxieties, when she became aware of panicked voices downstairs. She stilled, a chill sweeping over her as a horrible feeling filled her. She stood up slowly, made her way to her bedroom door, pulled it open, ignoring the lump in her throat, and slowly crept downstairs.

She didn't want to know what it was, but she moved down the steps all the same.

Maybe nothing was wrong. Maybe she was imagining it—she was tired, after all, it was getting late, and she was exhausted, drained, from all the drama she'd been dealing with lately. She wasn't thinking straight. This wasn't healthy. After her mother confirmed everything was fine, she'd go back upstairs and go to bed early. She straightened her posture, already feeling better at the prospect of the plan. Or maybe she'd just successfully blotted out the strange feeling for a moment.

She reached the kitchen. Her parents and Archer sat at the table, upset expressions covering their faces. The bad feeling returned.

"Mom?" She took a step forward, and then Archer spoke, his voice gruff. "It's your friend, Saige."

"My friend? What?"

Her eyes caught on something on the table.

A red flyer.

Red for withdrawal.

Someone she knew was being withdrawn.

Archer's words. One of her friends.

Mirren's words. *"It's not like I'm really worth anything to this world..."*

The picture connected in her mind so fast she felt dizzy. She sank into a seat, trying to regain her focus, regain herself. Stay calm, Saige. She opened her eyes and then closed them. She didn't want to know. She didn't want to know. She didn't want to know. If she ignored it, would it go away?

She opened her eyes and picked up the piece of paper, her heartbeat drowning all out other noises.

To the Pemberton Family:

It is with a sad, but grateful, heart we deliver the news of the withdrawal of an acquaintance of yours. We are sad for your loss, but we are grateful we have been able to weed out another delinquent and prevent more hurt from coming upon this community.

Name: Mirren Rebekah Chase
Level: 11
Score: Yellow
Time of arrest: Friday, September 12, 3:23pm. Reason: The subject was caught trying to escape our community.

We would like to inform you the withdrawal date will be Saturday, September 20, and the formal goodbye will be on Friday, September 19, at 12:00pm. You are welcome to attend.

Your daughter, Saige Raena Pemberton, qualifies for grieving schedules due to her connection with the subject.
We express our condolences and express our hopes that you find closure in the next two weeks. We also would like to remind you of withdrawal procedures. Once the two weeks are up, the subject will no longer exist to us. It is for the good of all of us here and the reason we have gotten thus far. We thank you for your cooperation in our community.

Department of Withdrawal, Community #12 September 13, Year 99

Saige felt sick.

"No," she said, choking on air.

Did that say a group of rebels?

She lifted the paper, and beneath were two more sheets identical to the first, with her ex-friends' names on them. Brightly. Marzia.

She couldn't breathe.

She had *known* something was off about Brightly.

Could this have been prevented if she had said something? And how did Mirren get herself entangled in this?

Falling to the ground, she pressed her hands to her eyes.

Sorrow twisted within her, but she didn't run to her room this time, where she could cry behind a closed door. She suddenly had no strength to even cry.

Mirren hated school. It was a blatant reminder in her face that she wasn't good enough. What was supposed to have helped her had failed her. She had done everything right, gotten high scores in all her classes, and look where it'd landed her—within inches of withdrawal. She wished she could find some way to just leave now.

Sure, she'd passed her test, but barely. She wasn't good enough to be here, had never been good enough to be here, and now the fact she was still here was only going to pull everyone down with her. She had successfully destroyed every relationship she'd had worth having—first Emory and Dawson, and now Risa and Saige. She was a walking disaster. She'd be better off to everyone if she was just withdrawn.

She'd been walking down the hall on the way to lunch, grumpy and upset, frustrated with herself and with the world, when, out of the corner of her eye, she'd seen some-one disappear down the end of a side hallway—one that definitely did not lead to the cafeteria. In a former time she would have ignored it, even reported it; but in a new reality where suddenly she didn't care, she found herself quickly running down the hall after them.

As she rounded the corner they swung around—two girls, one with freckles and curly hair, one with long black hair and dark eyes—panic coating their expression.

"Who are you?" the curly-haired one immediately demanded, stepping forward.

"Who are *you*?" Mirren retorted, adjusting the straps on her backpack. "I could report you right now, you know, for not following your schedule."

The girls exchanged looks, then the other one, the one with dark eyes, stepped forward, too, even closer to Mirren. "We asked you first," she hissed. "We could report you, too, you know."

"Go ahead." One of the many perks of not caring anymore. "My name is Mirren Chase. I'm eleventh level, and I'm Green." She held up her watch as evidence. "Your turn."

"You don't care about us potentially turning you in." It started as a question, but then became a statement. Mirren eyed the girl who spoke. "Not particularly. At the moment, I'm more curious about you."

The girls exchanged looks again. "Brightly Blackwell," the curly-haired girl said. "That's Marzia. We're eleventh level, too."

"Except we're Purple," said Marzia, smirking, and Brightly shot her an evil look. "You want to tick her off now, Marzia?"

"She doesn't looked ticked off to me." Marzia regarded Mirren warily. "Listen, what do you want?"

For a split second, something like regret and guilt coursed through her, but she pushed it aside. "What are you doing?"

"Why do you care? Just so you can report us?"

"I could already report you."

"Then what on earth are you doing?" Brightly sent her a long, exasperated look after nervously glancing behind her shoulder.

Marzia was looking nervous now, too. "Brights—"

"Marzia, I know. We have to get out of here. Girl, I'm giving you five seconds to explain what on earth you're trying to do now, and we're leaving, and trust me when I say if you try to follow you'll regret it. One—"

"Because I want in," Mirren blurted, and now both girls were looking at her. "You're obviously involved in something nonstandard. You're skipping schedule. I'm done with this world and its rules and ways. Whatever you're planning, I'm in."

Brightly stepped closer to her, then closer, studying her carefully. Mirren held her gaze as inside a battle raged, between her fear of what could happen to her if she did this, and desperation at the prospect living the rest of her life in this world that obviously didn't want her.

"Come with us, then," Brightly said after a long minute.

She turned and strode down the hallway, Marzia at her heels.

And after a split second of indecision, Mirren followed.

That had been two weeks ago now. Two weeks spent getting acquainted with Brightly, who was someone Mirren never would have spent time with before—deceitful, dishonest, and arrogant. Marzia was no better, but they were her key out of this place.

Brightly was done with this world, too. She wanted to see the world. She wanted to explore. But leaving the community with no intent to return was completely against standard, and something she could never acquire travel permissions for. Marzia agreed with her, and together, they'd apparently been planning a getaway for months.

"Once we're gone, nobody will come after us,"

Brightly explained to Mirren patiently. "We'll be too far gone for them to realistically find us, and they won't dare break standard themselves to stay out long enough to find us."

It seemed foolproof enough. And Mirren could see easily where Brightly got the notion that nobody cared. She doubted anyone would blink an eye over her disappearance.

Except maybe Saige. Her stomach twisted for a moment, recalling their angry conversation. No. Saige wouldn't care.

Nobody would care.

It had been all running according to plan. Their midnight planning sessions had come off smoothly, their secret protected by the cover of night, and the day had finally come to put it into action.

Mirren avoided her family during breakfast, and, as usual, they avoided her. At school, she avoided her friends. None of them tried to talk to her, either.

After school, she told her parents she was going to see Saige, and they lit up momentarily. "Oh, that's great, Mirren," her mother said absently. "Saige is a good friend."

For a second, Mirren considered the words, but then pushed them away. It was too late to back out now.

"Yeah," she said, feeling a sudden pang of sadness. Even if they did fight…Saige *had* been a good friend. She focused her energy on tying the final knot in her shoes. Did

Saige know how good of a friend she'd been?

"Have a good social," her mom called as she left.

"Bye," she called back, swallowing hard, knowing it was the last time she'd speak to her mother.

As she walked the path to Brightly's house, something welled up within her. It almost felt like sadness, but that was ridiculous. Nobody would care when she left; why should she care to leave them?

Taking a breath, she plowed forward, confidently putting one foot in front of the other. She was doing everyone a favor by disappearing.

But seeing the look of death from officials waiting for them just beyond the forest sent fear like she had never known shooting through her. It was one thing to plan an escape, and a whole another to watch the officers grab her friends, then her, pulling her back with a rough grip, hearing Marzia's screeching, seeing the look of anguish on Brightly's face.

But even then, she didn't feel guilty. Nor did she regret what she had done. The only thing she could feel was anger, slowly building within her, toward this world, toward her family and her friends, for not caring about what happened to her.

Anger because she definitely would now be leaving

the community, except to be sent to the Holding—the place she grew up terrified of. Now, instead of leaving a brave rebel, she would be leaving a defeated criminal.

After they had carted her and Brightly and Marzia back into town, past horrified passersby and into the courthouse, they pulled her aside into a confined room and proceeded to tell her that they had had tabs on Brightly and Marzia for months, but they had no idea how she had found them.

They were worried, they said, of how she found them, and if there could be more rebels lurking within their community. This was her chance, they told her. Her chance to do one last noble thing before being locked away for life. To end her life here on a positive note.

"Who told you where to find them, Chase?" they screamed at her when she wouldn't respond, mistakenly assuming she was keeping something from them. "Who else knows, Chase?"

And Mirren opened her mouth and all her rage and frustration exploded in just five words that would shatter what was left of her world she was leaving behind.

"It was Risa Dobbin, sir."

This wasn't happening.

Risa's mouth was dry. Her head was swimmy. Her legs were weak. Not now. No, please. Not Mirren.

"Withdrawal order?" Her father could speak, voicing the words taking over Risa's mind. Not Mirren.

Whatever if they hadn't been speaking to each other. That didn't mean that she never wanted to see her again.

"She was caught this afternoon with some rebels. Trying to escape." It was treason to leave the community without a written passport; after all, it basically communicated one didn't like their city, and that was treasonous.

How could the official's voice be so calm? Could he not see he was destroying what was left of her world with each word? She fought to digest his meaning. With *rebels*?

Mirren—caught with rebels?

"And that's what I'm here about, Miss Dobbin."

Why did his tone change? Did he have so little empathy to not realize the weight of the news he had just delivered? In a different situation, Risa might have scoffed at him. "There have been reportings of noises in the night lately. People have been hearing weird things. We hadn't really looked into it, but we got more complaints, so we started investigating. After a few weeks of this, we narrowed down who it was and caught them this afternoon. It was a group of girls, who have been wandering about after curfew. Plotting."

Those had been *Mirren's* footsteps she heard?

"Ridiculous girls. They think they can get away with anything. They've been plotting what they call ah, let's see, an escape. According to our investigation so far, they have been up for this for who knows how long, though it does seem Miss Chase only joined them recently, if that is of any comfort. Either way, we were ready for them when they ran today. Fortunately, we were able to apprehend all three of them."

He narrowed his eyes to meet Risa's, and she felt chills suddenly rush up her spine. "All three have been sentenced to withdrawal. But that's not why I'm here." He held her gaze, and she trembled. "Miss Dobbin, we have reason to suspect there could be more of our own citizens working against us in this way, and we have reason to believe you may be one of them. Do you deny this claim?"

"What?" cried Risa, blinking. "What? Of course not! I mean, of course I do! I didn't even know they existed!"

"Miss Dobbin, the one thing we could not figure out is how Miss Chase became associated with these top-secret rebels. She told us that you were the link to finding them." His words were sharp now, his gaze even more piercing.

"No…" The word was a fragile breath.

"Protocol is to mistrust rebels, but—"

"No!" Risa screamed, and his eyes widened at her interruption. "I'm not a rebel! I never spoke a word to these so-called rebels! I didn't even know they existed!"

"I am obliged to believe you," the law official said, and suddenly he became twice as intimidating as he took a step toward her. "But this is a matter of utmost security, and for safety reasons, I also am obliged to take you in until we can prove you were not involved."

Risa stared blankly at him, fury kindling within her as he led her out of her own house as a prisoner, fury so hot it quickly overtook the sadness until all she could feel was the terrible anger throbbing in her head, becoming worse and worse with every second.

Saige struggled her way down the street, trying to stand straight, trying to get a grip on her life, because it felt like it was slipping away before her eyes. She just wanted Mirren.

Why hadn't she done more? Why hadn't she been a better friend?

Why did the world have to be this way?

Mirren wasn't a criminal.

Except somehow she was.

Her friend's words echoed in her mind on endless repeat: "*Maybe I don't want you to be my friend.*"

She got back home way after dinner had started and ended, and yet, when Archer and her parents pounced on her, demanding to know where she'd been, she couldn't recall the afternoon at all.

"Saige," her father said at the start of family time,

slowly and carefully. Her thoughts felt blurry. "I don't want to know whatever you're going to tell me."

"She accused Risa, sweetie," her mother said as Saige started to turn away; as soon as the words were out of her mouth Saige spun back around. "What?"

"We thought....we thought you should know." Her mother looked worn out, like she already regretted telling Saige. "They had to pull Risa in for questioning. I'm sorry, honey."

"What?" Saige exclaimed, mind spinning. "What? But Risa's innocent!" *Wasn't* she?

She *was* innocent, right?

She had to be. Unless the two of them had been plotting this all along....

Bitterness swirled in her stomach, creating a nauseating feeling. She pushed it aside. No; Risa didn't do this. She was better than this.

But only a few weeks ago, she would have said the same about Mirren.

Memories buzzed in her head, from when she first met the two of them, how much fun they'd had together, to the many long and hard conversations she'd had with Mirren this year, and soon her mind became overrun by her friend's harsh, horrible, sickening words.

"Maybe I don't want you to be my friend."

"It's not like I'm really worth anything to this world."

It doesn't matter.

She was haunted by her hopelessness and suddenly wondered if this was how Mirren had felt, all these months.

All of this didn't matter.

What did it matter, the good times and the bad times they had had?

What did it matter what she could have done? There was nothing she could do now.

She had to say goodbye to Mirren.

After September nineteenth, she'd never see her again.

They wouldn't let her see Mirren. Saige went to the law office, begged them, but they refused. Of course they did. She knew they would; it was standard. Association with criminals—withdrawees—outside of the goodbye ceremony was not appropriate.

She couldn't picture Mirren as one of those evil criminals, the ones she read about in books who were crooked from birth, who plotted out malicious plans and just waited for the moment to put them into action. That couldn't be Mirren.

That had never been Mirren.

That would never be Mirren.

Could it?

"Maybe I don't want you to be my friend."

She thought back to their friendship this summer, how different Mirren had become, how strange she had acted. Maybe she hadn't been herself, but that didn't mean she had become a threat—did it? That didn't mean she would have become dangerous—did it?

Except she *was* dangerous. She had tried to rebel. Was no one allowed a second chance?

She already knew the answer. She'd been taught it her whole life. Second chances were more dangerous than the actual criminals.

She slid to the ground, her back pressed against the office's front door. Only feet from her, her best friend sat imprisoned.

How had nobody seen this coming?

Why was it everyone Saige loved got taken from her?

"Excuse me, miss?"

It was a law officer, having opened the door to find Saige sitting motionless outside. "Do you need something?"

She leapt to her feet, renewed determination filling her. "I want to see my friend," she said. "Mirren Chase. She's not a criminal."

"I'm afraid she is," said the officer, "or she wouldn't be here."

"You don't know Mirren," Saige said, blinking rapidly. "She made a mistake, but this isn't who she is."

"I'm sorry," said the officer. "We don't have time to figure out who she is. All that matters is what she did."

"No," Saige whispered, watching him go, anger filling her at the futility of her words. "That's not all that matters."

Emory found her one day after school. She must have come home from High Honor. Which of course she did—she couldn't miss saying goodbye to her sister for the last time.

But even Saige knew the complications leaving for so long would have on her High Honor progress.

How could Mirren have done this?

"Saige," she said without emotion. "I'm supposed to ask you to read at...my sister's ceremony." Her words sickened Saige, like she couldn't even bring herself to say Mirren's name.

"Her name is Mirren," Saige said, equally as emotionlessly. "And of course I'll read. Do I have a choice?"

· ·

She laid in bed in the darkness of night, listening to the nothingness everywhere and being unable to rid herself of the knowledge that after tomorrow's ceremony, Mirren would be gone—gone forever.

And there was nothing to do about it.

Except follow grieving schedules.

And then let go. Move on. Like her friend had never existed.

So what if they'd fought? One fight, even one bad summer, didn't erase all the good memories. She didn't want to let it erase the Mirren she remembered, but already she felt weary. Society was already doing that for her.

Mirren is not the kind of person who should be withdrawn from society.

She is the kind of person this society needs.

Saige knew her thoughts were not following standard, but she needed them.

"Maybe I don't want you to be my friend."

"It's not like I'm really worth anything to this world."

Saige lifted her head from her desk and found herself with a pounding headache. Had she really dozed off that much?

Why could she not get ahold of herself?

Might as well start on that goodbye piece. The poem she'd read to let everyone know she was done with Mirren and she was letting her go.

She picked out a blue pen and opened her notebook, flipped on her desk light. She poised the pen over the paper, stone-faced, and couldn't find a single word to write.

She couldn't do this.

She dropped the pen, got up and paced around her room, found a picture pinned to her bulletin board of her and Mirren at the skating rink. She pulled it off to look at it: Mirren's blonde hair falling out of its braids, her friend's smile bright. Saige herself was blurry, mid-laugh as she probably was mid-fall.

A week ago the picture would have brought a smile to her lips. Today nothing about her expression changed.

She stared stone-faced at the picture for a long, long moment, then out of nowhere with a surge of emotion ripped it in half.

She stared at the halves in her hand, felt her heart pounding in her ears, watched the pieces drift from her hand to the floor, and as they dropped emotion welled up within her and she sank to her knees, grabbing them back with shaking hands.

How perfect a job she had done—the tear went right between her and Mirren.

Separating them.

Her fingers trembled, and suddenly she knew what she would write for the poem, though with every word she had to lie to herself that this was just a gift to her friend and not the final words she'd ever say to her, and that the parts of the page that were soaked through were because she spilled water and not because of her tears she'd been unable to stop.

They questioned Risa for hours, right there in the law office, the place they only brought criminals. And here she was, spending hours here. Anger stewed within her with each passing minute. Who did Mirren think she was, to do this to her? What had she ever done to Mirren except be her friend?

She stated the truth to the officials over and over until she felt like she could do in her sleep. Mindlessly reciting things left lots of time to fester her anger toward Mirren.

"You only care about yourself and your pithy problems..."

"I don't care about your problems anymore, Risa."

Eventually, they let her go to bed, but not bed in her own home, but bed, here in the office, overnight, the same place where they kept criminals, until they could confirm her story. They promised her over and over they believed her, but there were "protocols" to follow. Risa had stopped listening to them long ago.

By the time they let her go to her cot—at least it was in a room and not a locked cell—with an encouragement that it would end up in her favor, she didn't care anymore. She still had to spend a night in this rotten place.

She got on her cot and pulled the blanket up over her head, descending into desperate, angry tears which eventually gave way to the nothingness of sleep.

She dreamt of Mirren. She dreamt of swimming at the pool with her, or skating, or going to see movies, or just hanging out together at her house. She dreamt of her friend's sweet laugh, her encouraging smile, the uncanny way she always knew when Risa needed a hug (though Risa would never admit it).

But then her dreams changed and suddenly she was dreaming of Brynlee—she dreamed, over and over, of that moment when she held her sister's hand as Brynlee fought for life. She woke and fell back to sleep again and again, unsure of reality.

She saw Mirren in her dreams, sitting outside her house on the doorstep for hours, day after day, but when Risa tried to talk to her, Mirren screamed, "I don't care about your pithy problems!"

In other dreams, Mirren said, "When I get withdrawn, Risa, do you know what everybody's going to say? They're going to say, 'She's had that coming a long time.'"

Risa woke suddenly, panic filling her. The air around her was cold and haunting, and she shivered.

She felt oddly that something had awoken her, but she didn't know what. Involuntarily she recalled the events of the day, saw them happen in slow motion in her mind, and her anger was kindled again. All their years of friendship—for this?

She stared up into the blackness, fists clenched, and then she heard it. A small sound from across the building, penetrating the silence. It sounded like someone crying, and Risa instantly knew who it was.

Stealthily, Risa got out of bed, pulling her blanket with her around her shoulders, ignoring the tears still freely falling down her face—but she was mad at Mirren, she was furious, Mirren had betrayed her—and stepped out of her small room. She followed the sound until she reached the hall of holding cells. Slowly she crept down the hall until she stopped in front of one of the heavy doors. She sank to her knees, pressing her ear to the door, and heard louder than ever before her best friend's sobs.

Pressing her hand against the heavy door, cried silently, unmoving, for a long time, agony and anger mixing together in her mind until she wasn't sure of anything she was feeling. After what felt like hours she rose to her feet and tried the door, remembering learning somewhere that they were designed so you could get in, but not out. The heavy door slid open with a creak, and she stepped forward, shaking, unsure why she was here.

Mirren: curled up in a ball on the cot, her hair everywhere, covered in dirt and scrapes and bruises, sobbing so hard. When she heard the door open she shot upward and her eyes widened when she saw Risa.

Risa stood in the doorway, expressionless, pulling the blanket tight around her, staring at her friend, and

Mirren stared back at her.

No *I'm sorry*. Nothing but silence.

Risa swallowed. She didn't speak. They stayed like that for a long, hard, awful moment.

"I never want to see you again," Risa finally said.

She didn't wait around to see her friend's reaction.

PART 6

PART 6

Callum Andrews swept past the schedule. No one followed the schedules anymore. He completely ignored it as he left his room.

Okay, maybe it was a cell. He preferred to think of it as his room. It made life more bearable. Less—depressing. Maybe he was the only one who thought this way, but it was better than being upset all the time.

He exited the building, greeting Brecken and Blaze, who watched over the building at night. Others might call it guarding. Callum preferred to think of it as watching over. It sounded less—*threatening*. Besides, it wasn't like the brothers were mean, cruel outsiders; they were withdrawees, too, and just happened to be assigned the guarding duty ahead of Callum, who, even after being here a whole eight years, was still on the youth scheduling. Good thing nobody actually followed the schedules.

Oh, the schedules were real, put in place by real officials who ran the place from afar, coming in only once every season to stamp the schedules on the walls of every room. Those were scary days, and no one ever knew when they came either, thanks to the lack of calendar. People here had tried to put one into place, but it was too hard to get everyone motivated to keep it going. To Callum, it didn't matter. Days were days, and that was it.

He had finally reached a point where he was okay with this place. In some ways it was worse than he feared, but in other ways it was better. For one, he had pictured, in his young mind—for he had been six years old when he was withdrawn—he had pictured huge, threatening guards stomping around, keeping everyone in order. But there was virtually no one from the outside here. It was said there were guards outside the walls, but the walls were so high that nobody really knew if that was true, and if it was, where they were. As a result, there was a haphazard type of community that had forged its way into existence.

He had also been surprised by the amount of kind people here. He had imagined everyone being ruthless criminals, but it wasn't true. And due to lack of outside in-fluence, a lot of them managed to retain that spark of kind-ness. Many here, after all, were just low scorers, those who weren't smart enough for their world, and some had been withdrawn due to bad health. There were, of course, truly dangerous people here too, though, and there had been times when they rose to power—completely a result of lack of authority. Authority was a constant battle being fought here.

But anyway, it wasn't too bad. Mostly, though, in Callum's opinion, because of the lack of outside authority enforcing the rules. If he had to follow the schedule posted in his room, he could imagine becoming deeply miserable very fast. But thankfully, the rest of the world remained scared of them, and they were left alone.

Outside of the large, intimidating wall locking them inside, outside of all the intense work they had to do to survive—again, another byproduct of nonexistent outside intervention, for they had to do everything themselves— outside of the few people living here that were worth fearing, outside of being separated forever from his family—outside of all that, it was actually okay, living here in the Holding.

But then again, Callum was known for his extreme sense of optimism.

He made his way to the cafeteria building, enjoying the fresh air. During the winter simply walking between buildings was torture, with the lack of winter gear provided for them; but today, with the weather warm and comforting—it was actually nice.

He entered the building and headed to the kitchen, where he found the head cook, Elliott, waiting. "Need any help?"

"We're good today, Callum." The cook managed a tight smile.

"Sounds good." He turned and left, intending to find a table with someone new to talk to. Callum had found a stash of paper and pens in a back room a few years earlier, and he used it to write down everything he could—daily journals, charts of necessary information, people's stories. Especially people's stories. He had whole boxes full of papers on the stories of people here, and he made clear to those who knew him that they were welcome to look through it whenever. Many did.

"Callum," someone said, and he looked over. It was Cassie, the girl he had talked to yesterday. Cassie had been withdrawn in First Level for a low score, and Callum thought it one of the worst mistakes their world had ever made. Cassie, despite growing up here, had a unique determination many others didn't, and she still had quite the spunk, and she naturally also carried a maturity about her. She was ten years old, but she could easily have been much older. Interviewing her had been a highlight of the week for Callum.

Now, he walked over to her, smiled. "What's up?"

"Do you think there'll be any newbies this year?" she asked him. "Are we ready for it?"

Callum was still confused why everyone came to him with these questions. "I guess we are. We have plenty of empty rooms still in the children's building, but the main center is filling up. We may need to build an extension." He winced as he said it. Building an extension would take a long time and lots of labor. "I was hoping to push it off till next year."

"I know we all were," she replied, then she asked eagerly, "Has there been any reports of anyone coming near?"

Callum, last year, had instituted a watch during this time of year—late summer—the time when the most new arrivals came in. He'd helped construct a ladder up the towering walls, and designated watchmen would climb up every so often, checking for any incoming vehicles that would signify authority was on its way. When he'd proposed the idea, everyone had been exuberant, and now they were anxious for it to pay off again. This past spring, when a few new withdrawees had arrived, it had been a success—everyone was able to be ready and prepared, and since the enthusiasm for it had only increased.

"Not yet," he said. "I'll check again after we eat. I'll find you later, okay?"

"Okay," she said, shrugging as he left.

"Callum!"

He was on his way to check on the children's building when he heard his name and turned to see one of the watchmen running toward him. "We see the van," he panted. "It's probably ten minutes off."

Callum nodded, slowly at first but then faster as the words registered in his mind. "Okay. Help spread the word. Thank you!"

"Shouldn't everyone probably go back to their cells?" the watchman asked, worriedly.

"No," Callum said, shaking his head. "We've been out and about every time they arrive and they've never done anything about it."

"True, but will they tolerate it forever?" the watchmen said worriedly.

"Suddenly being on schedule in our rooms when they arrive will give away that we somehow knew they were coming," Callum said. "I think that's more dangerous for us than just being out, like we've been for years."

"Right," said the watchman finally, and then dashed off to help spread the word.

Callum continued walking to the children's building, picking up his pace. His heart was beating rapidly, too. Newcomers were always hit or miss. This could just be a group of poor low-scorers, failing to pass their re-test after being marked orange. But every so often there was what

Callum thought of as a true criminal—someone withdrawn for other reasons than just intelligence or health. And that, they never knew ahead of time. He hated the unknown; it scared him. He disliked the helplessness of it. But it was just the life he had to lead now.

He notified the leaders of the children's building and then headed back outside, where he kept a corner of his eye trained on the one entrance, the one that locked from the outside, the one they couldn't barrel down no matter what they tried. The one constant reminder that no matter how kind they were to one another, no matter what community they forged, no matter what they did, they were still prisoners and they were still under the fist of someone above them.

Callum wouldn't wish this life on anyone. And yet, every year, he had to stand by and watch as the outside world forced more and more people in, for mostly ridiculous and cruel reasons, and he could do nothing about it except at least try to make life inside bearable.

So that's what he did. He never referred to their cells as such if he could help it. He helped institute a watch to give them sort of advance notice. He took newcomers under his wing—the innocent ones, kicked out of their worlds for what he thought no reason—and helped them adjust. He did his best to negotiate with the more violent personalities and keep them from hurting others. He organized workers to help sort and organize the food that was shipped to them, and he had helped plant the grove of fruit trees that would one day blossom and provide them with their own source of food. He guessed he had sort of become their leader, though he didn't like the title and didn't understand why.

He was only fifteen.

When the huge door rolled aside and the van drove slowly in, Callum was ready, watching from behind the cafeteria building. They had learned it was never good to be around when the newcomers arrived. The people bringing them tended to be rough and merciless. There'd be plenty of time to help the newcomers later, once their captors left.

He watched, eyes narrowed, hidden from sight as three girls climbed out of the vehicle. Three. He knew that for the world they'd come from, three was a lot. In the spring, yes, there were usually quite a few of them. But three for this time of year was almost unheard of.

They all looked around his age. He regarded them warily as their captors started to corral them to the dormitory building while barking rules at them. None of the rules were actually heeded, but the newcomers had yet to learn that.

Callum's heart panged for them. They didn't know it'd be okay here. They were probably scared to death, just like he had been. There was just no way to reveal anything with the outside authority here.

After the van left an hour later, he headed over the building with a few others following behind, and went upstairs, where he knew the only empty rooms were.

He crept up silently, not wanting to scare them, and penetrating the silence was the sound of someone crying. He was used to seeing this hopelessness in newcomers, and it never ceased to make him hurt inside. They shouldn't be here.

He walked to the first door, opened it up. The girl inside was straight-faced and almost indignant. Whatever. She'd lose that feeling of superiority soon. At least, hopefully she would. Callum really didn't want to deal with a troublesome teen.

Leaning against the doorway, he studied her. "What's your name?" he asked.

She jumped a little and crossed her arms. "Who are you?" she demanded suspiciously. "Why should I tell you?"

Callum didn't have time for this. He left her door open and went on to the next room. The girl inside looked relieved, but wouldn't speak to him. "Go ahead and go wherever you like," he invited her finally. "There'll be people down on the grounds to explain and all."

Behind the last door was a girl sitting on the floor, her back pressed against the wall and her face buried in her knees, shaking.

Callum didn't know what to do. "Hello?" he finally said.

She jerked her face up. "Who are you?" Her voice wobbled as she wiped her eyes and sniffled, as if she was trying to stop crying, though if she was, it wasn't working. He cleared his throat. "I'm Callum."

"Are you in charge here or something?" Her voice was quiet.

He shrugged. "I guess," he said, studying her. "Who are you?"

She looked away and swallowed. "It doesn't matter," she finally said, avoiding his eyes.

Callum waited a moment and tried again. Something about her intrigued him. "What's your name?"

"Mirren," she said dully.

"Well...Mirren. Welcome, I guess. You're welcome to leave whenever. This place...it's not as bad as you think. You won't be locked in your room, at least."

She still didn't meet his eyes. "Alright."

"Do you want to come outside?" he invited. "I could introduce you to some people." She didn't seem to be in the greatest shape, and he'd sleep better if he could find her someone to watch out for her.

Her eyes still avoiding him, she muttered, "Okay," and then silently stood up and followed him down.

· ·

He took her first to the cafeteria, where she replied to his introductions and explanations with grunts. He had expected her to perk up at the relief it wasn't a cruel prison, but she showed no sign of any emotion at all, just mindlessly followed him. But, he supposed, that wasn't too atypical. He didn't know why suddenly it was so important to him that she was okay. All newcomers took a while to adjust. He knew this.

He brought her around the rest of the grounds as he typically did, pointing out the section to stay away from where the more violent personalities lived, showing her the children's building and the beginnings of the fruit tree grove and the storage building, looking closely at her for any type of response, but there was nothing.

Finally she asked him if she could just go back to her cell.

"I prefer to think of it as a room, not a cell," he said. "But sure."

"And I can just come out whenever I want?" she said, eyeing him warily.

All this time spent explaining the world, and she

still doubted his integrity? He shook his head, clearing his mind. Again, this was not atypical. Why was it bothering him this time?

"Yes. Just come down whenever. Brecken and Blaze are the appointed watch for our building, but they know you're not dangerous so they won't give you a problem." Not that they really could do anything if she was dangerous, but just their presence provided the rest of them a peace of mind.

Mirren nodded, breathed in, and turned back towards the building. Callum watched her walk away, saw the way she lowered her head as she went, and he wondered for not the first time what on earth had gotten her here. Somehow, a low score just didn't seem like the cause this time.

⋯⋯⋯●●●●●●●●●●●●●●●●●●●●●●●●●⋯⋯

She couldn't find any hope left in her. Whether or not the Holding was some terrifying, awful place, or someplace bearable, like Callum insisted, didn't matter to her anymore. She obviously deserved the first option, but she also selfishly was glad when it didn't come to pass. Selfish. That's all she was.

She became numb. Mindlessly doing whatever Callum asked to her, whether it was to eat something, or volunteer for something, or help him with something. She would have been touched by his interest in her in another life, but not now. It didn't matter anymore. No one deserved her as a friend. Not after what she did.

Days passed by.

 Days turned into weeks.

 Weeks turned into months.

 Mirren was gone.

Two awful months later, Saige decided she was sick of being miserable.

 So she zipped up her jacket, took a deep breath, and left the house.

 Mirren's departure would stay with her for life. She knew it in her bones, but that wasn't what she was upset about. She couldn't forget Mirren, but more, she would never choose to. She still clung to the memories with ferocity, determined to never let them fade. She wasn't about to go along with society and pretend Mirren never existed. Her step faltered as the thought crossed her mind, but she forced her steps back in line. She was going to keep moving.

Her sweet friend had impacted her life so much; she could at least keep going with the Saige that Mirren had helped her become and not completely throw away the part of her that she knew somehow, someway, had been shaped by her friendship with Mirren.

She wasn't going to let Mirren's withdrawal get in the way of being the best Saige she could be. So she started thinking. She couldn't make things right with Brightly, because first of all, that was a friendship she knew she had to let go of, and secondly, because Brightly had been withdrawn. Mirren was gone too, and she'd tried to reach Risa to no avail. But there was someone else who Saige owed an apology, someone she should have apologized to long ago.

So she walked the streets briskly in the spring weather, her heart thumping with each step, reminding herself with each breath that she could do this.

She didn't have to abandon her goals of being the Saige she wanted to be just because she didn't have a best friend anymore. Her step faltered again, and she stopped, closed her eyes, and took another breath, in, out, before going on.

Saige turned the corner and took a breath again.

None of her other friends had ever lived down this street; she hadn't been down here in over a year. Her feet still knew the way.

She reached the door, heaved one more breath, and

then thudded on the door, once, twice. After a long minute the door creaked open and Saige found herself face to face with Linley Andrews.

Also known as her former best friend.

The last time they had talked—nearly two years ago—Saige had yelled at her that she never wanted to talk to her again.

Much like how one of her last conversations with Mirren had gone. But this was one situation she could fix.

Linley leaned against the doorframe, regarding her with a heavy gaze. Saige met her eyes, unafraid. "Linley. I came here because I wanted to—tell you something."
Linley held the gaze a moment, and then crossed her arms.

Here we go. "Linley, I'm sorry. I messed up with you. I shouldn't have ditched you on Holiday and I definitely shouldn't have said the things I said to you when you tried to talk to me." She talked fast, hoping her words were coming out the way she had arranged them in her mind. "I just needed to tell you I'm sorry. I know it's kind of really late, but I'm trying to become a better friend, and I just needed you to know—you know—I don't think bad of you or anything—I want to be a better friend to you—" She searched for words, hoping she was correctly communicating her heart.

Linley listened to her until she finished, looking up at her wordlessly, and then, much to Saige's surprise, she rushed forward. "I missed you, Saige," she said, squeezing her tightly.

"I—I miss you, too." Saige hadn't realized it until she said it.

If only her sadness over Mirren could be solved so simply.

"I'm sorry, too," Linley said, pulling away and looking at her. "I haven't exactly been super nice to you in response."

Saige shrugged, not finding it a problem. "You had every right."

Linley looked at her quizzically for a long moment.

"Can I ask you a question? What made you decide to come talk to me?"

Of course she would ask. That was Linley—straightforward about everything. Saige didn't want to tell her. But she couldn't lie. "Linley, did you know Mirren Chase?"

Linley's forehead crinkled. "I know of her. She was—she was one who was withdrawn, right?"

"Yeah. She is—she was—pretty much my best friend." She saw Linley stiffen at her use of the word and tried to quickly correct herself. "She kinda pulled me back onto the right path, if you know what I mean. Anyway—well—since, you know, she...left...I just felt like...what kind of person was I if I—just abandoned who I was becoming just because she left?" Was she making any sense? Probably not, but Linley was looking at her like she understood.

"I get you," she said softly. "I'm really sorry to hear that. Mirren was such a kind girl." Her look darkened. "We aren't supposed to say that, are we?"

Probably not. "It's fine. She was."

"I remember," Linley said, picking at a hangnail, "last year, I was having a rough day and forgot my lunch. I'm—well, I was—at her same table, and when she saw me freaking out, she just took out half her lunch and gave it to me so that to any school officials who came by it would seem like both of us were just half-finished." Her look darkened again. "Saige, what happened? No one told me the whole story." Then a panicked expression came across her face, and she backpedaled. "You don't have to tell me."

Saige swallowed and looked away. "She scored Orange in the spring," she finally said, "and we—well, we think that's what started it, but she scored fine on the retake..." She trailed off, her tongue feeling thick in her mouth. Green wasn't fine. It was barely passing-grade. "She was caught with rebels outside the city boarders and then she falsely accused her other—my other—close friend." She closed her eyes. "Risa—Risa Dobbin."

When she opened her eyes again, she saw the deep sadness in Linley's eyes. "That's awful," she said, sniffling. "That explains a lot, too."

Saige shook her head. "Explains what?" What would Linley know that she didn't about Mirren?

"Risa—oh, I shouldn't tell you this, Saige." Linley looked away, her eyes brimmed with tears, then back at Saige. "The rumors have been that Risa's on her own way to withdrawal. Ever since Mirren—left, she degraded really fast, apparently. She talks to no one and her school performance has plummeted."

Saige felt her heart beat, beat, beat in her ears with each word Linley said.

"It wasn't just Mirren," she blurted. "Risa's sister died at the beginning of the summer."

Now Linley's eyes bugged out, and she opened her mouth, but before she could speak, Saige shook her head. "I—I have to go," she said, standing up and looking around but not moving, feeling more and more hopeless, helpless, with each passing second. Risa wouldn't get withdrawn. Not Risa, too. If Risa—

But even she had seen the affects of the summer begin to take a toll on Risa in the few times she'd encountered her unsmiling friend. And she could remember with terrifying clarity how she'd thought the same about Mirren—that she'd be fine.

And to Risa, she realized, withdrawal might not even be punishment. She'd at least get to see one of the people she lost again.

Saige's heart thumped within her. That still didn't make it right.

She felt the hopelessness consuming her.

"There's nothing we can do," she whispered, more to herself than Linley. "There's literally nothing I can do but watch as they take all the people who mean anything to me away from me for literally no reason."

She wanted to scream.

"I just need hope," she sniped.

"Saige," Linley said quickly. "Don't tell yourself that. There's always hope." But even then her voice shook a bit, like she was having to tell herself that, too.

"No, there's not," Saige said bitterly, running her hand down her hair and then pressing a hand to her face. "There's no hope for Mirren. No hope for Brynlee. No hope for Cassie. No hope for me." She hated everything. She hated everyone. She hated this awful world and she hated these awful rules and she wished she could just curl up somewhere and disappear forever.

"Oh, Saige," cried Linley, stepping forward, but Saige pushed her away. "Leave me alone." She needed to leave, but her legs wouldn't work.

"Just think," Linley begged through tearful eyes. "Oh, there has to be something we can do! Just think with me for a minute, Saige!"

"Why do you even care?" Saige exclaimed. "You

don't know Mirren or Risa anyone."

"I know you," Linley said.

"Like that matters," Saige muttered.

"Saige, what did you always tell me?" Linley cried, meeting Saige's eyes and grabbing her hand. "What did you always tell me, when I was discouraged about testing or whatever? You always told me, 'Linley, nothing you do changes how much you matter.' That goes for you, too!"

"But what about things I don't do?" Saige replied indignantly, shaking Linley's hand off.

"Okay, like what?" demanded Linley. "You apologized to me, a year and a half later. That takes guts, Saige. You seem to have been a great friend to Mirren and Risa—"

"Not that it matters," Saige said.

"Of course it matters!" Linley exclaimed. "Would you rather Mirren had an awful life here, too? What else, Saige? What have you not done that you think defines you?" Her words were weak, but something in them resonated with Saige.

"I didn't save my friend in time," she blurted. "I failed Mirren. She needed a friend, and I wasn't there for her. I didn't check on her enough. I wasn't a good enough friend." She blinked away sudden tears. Why on earth was she crying in front of Linley, now of all times?

"Saige, that's—I'm sure that's not true."

"It doesn't matter," Saige said again. "It's not like I

can fix it."

She turned to go, but Linley reached out and stopped her. "That isn't the Saige I know."

Saige stopped. Turned back around. "What?"

"This isn't the Saige I remember. Hopelessly giving up without even trying?"

"But I have tried, Linley. I—"

"Since she left. What have you tried since she left, Saige? You want things to be different…they can be different. Look at you. You just came and apologized to me. That shows your courage. Surely that took more courage than it would take to do something for Mirren."

"But like what?" Saige cried, swallowing. "What exactly can I do for Mirren? This world wants me to believe she never even existed."

"But she does exist," Linley replied, her voice barely over a whisper. "And that changes things, doesn't it?"

Then suddenly, up her spine, a tingling feeling, a weird feeling in her stomach, a sudden realization. Her sour attitude melted.

"Linley," she said, then swallowed and looked up at the sky.

"Yeah?"

"What if," she said, then stopped. She was going to sound like a rebel. But she had never heard of this, so maybe no else had ever thought of it, either, and consequently maybe there were no standards against it.

So maybe there was a chance. Maybe there was hope. Maybe she could do something.

"What if I went to the Holding and brought Mirren back?" she said.

Linley's face was grave, but her eyes were burning with passion.

"There's the Saige I know," she whispered.

"Saige, you *are* aware that there are standards against that." Risa held Saige's gaze, challenging her, daring her to keep talking. It was a foolish idea, and faulty through and through. She didn't know how Saige didn't see it.

And anyway, she never wanted to see Mirren again.

When Saige didn't reply right away, she turned her back and started to walk away. "We have lunch to get to, Saige. School won't stop for your silly ideas." She fast-walked down the hall, but Saige wouldn't give up. She ran after Risa, grabbed the hood of her sweater. "Risa, please, hear me out," she begged breathlessly. "Risa, please, you're my last hope."

"Then just accept the fact you're hopeless." The words were bitter on Risa's tongue.

Saige shook her head. "Please." Desperation crept into her voice, and despite the fact she was going to make them both late for lunch, Risa stopped walking, heaved a sigh loudly, and looked at Saige expectantly.

"I've done my research, Risa." Her words were animated, rushed. "I talked to my brother. He wants to do law work when he graduates. No one has ever tried to go to the Holding before. I—"

"And there's a reason for that, Saige," Risa shot back, her expression disgusted. "Personally, I'd like to remain as far away from all those criminals as possible. Including Mirren," she added indignantly when Saige opened her mouth to speak.

Saige shook her head again. "But what if Mirren's not a criminal?" she said carefully, watching closely for Risa's reaction.

"Mirren is a criminal," said Risa, crossing her arms tighter around herself. "Or did you forget what she did?"

Saige looked at a loss for words. "Risa. There are standards that say if a person commits an act against standards, or if they are too sick, or if they don't score high enough, they are withdrawn. There is no standards regarding what happens to that person if they return."

"That's because there's a reason nobody has ever returned," Risa replied, exasperated.

"But now there is a reason for someone to return," Saige said, her hopeful eyes pleading with Risa to understand. "So you're going to go and bring her back? How, exactly, do you plan to do this? How will you get there? How will you get in? And how do you know they won't just ship her back when you get back? Won't that be even worse?" Risa could think of a million problems. Her words tasted sour in her mouth.

"I don't know they won't send her back," Saige said, her gaze dropping for a fraction of a second. "But there's no standard regarding it. Which means it could go either way. And isn't it worth the risk that we might get our friend back? Her family could get their daughter and sister back?"

"And what if not? You're gonna work her all up and get your hopes sky-high, only for her to be sent away again? This is selfish."

"Selfish? Trying to break my best friend out of the Holding to bring her back to her family? Yeah, it's totally all for me." Saige looked at her in disbelief, and her voice became quiet. "I'm going, Risa. I was hoping you might come with me."

"I don't want to see Mirren ever again," Risa said, avoiding Saige's eyes.

Saige was quiet.

"You don't mean that," she said.

"I do mean it," Risa shot back. "Besides, why you for this? What makes your and friendship so special" —she emphasized the word—"that you have to go down in history for it?"

"You know what, Risa, fine," Saige said, heaving a

sigh, "fine."

"Oh, and Saige?" Risa called after Saige as she tromped back down the hall, her eyes downcast, shoulders slumped. The words were sharp in her mouth. "When you do find Mirren, because you obviously will, make sure to tell her that I hope I never talk to her again."

Saige didn't reply. Risa crossed her own arms tightly across her chest as she walked away, fighting sobs the entire way.

The arrival of night brought with it dreams of things she had wished to put far from her mind, of emotions she wished to keep tucked away, of fears that had ruled her life.

She had survived this far, but now sudden terror consumed her as memories she had hoped to forget suddenly made their reappearance in her mind. Mirren sank in and out of sleep, reality and dream blurring together until all she could feel was the emotion that ran deep within her bones, and the pain, the sorrow, the intense agony and regret, and the sudden illogical longing for those she'd never see again—for they wouldn't want to see her.

She jerked awake halfway through the night in a cold sweat, the thought twisting its painful path through her mind as unshed tears burned in her eyes. Who was she? Who had she become? Panic seized her as once more the gravity of her surroundings attacked her—how had she gotten here? Why was she here? She shouldn't be here. She should be home—with Emory—Dawson—Risa—Saige—

She tugged the threadbare sheet over her head and curled into a ball, her breathing labored as sudden exhaustion overtook her—or maybe her body was just shutting down in attempt to avoid the reality around her— sending her back to reside in the deep pain that was her dreams.

She was at Dawson's wedding again, spinning in the glittery dress that made her feel like a princess. She was walking down the aisle ahead of her sister-in-law, loving and hating the attention. Exchanging silly glances with Saige during the ceremony. She remembered the fleeting feeling of pure happiness in those moments, those moments when she still felt hopeful, that everything was going to turn out all right.

Then she was in First Level again, feeling the icky feeling of fear creep its way through her as memories that hadn't dared to show themselves before replayed over and over in her mind.

And then suddenly the memories morphed into ones of this past summer, ones where she heard the announcer read off her Orange score, and both memories— of First Level and of this year—brought back the sickening feeling she experienced looking around and seeing the scared, horrified looks on people's faces, like she was some sort of criminal.

Everyone had been so pityingly kind to her family, even back in First Level, but no one had ever spoken to her.

Like they assumed withdrawal was her destiny.

Even at five years old, nobody believed in her.

Saige drifted her way into dreams that were happy and heartbreaking all at once, for even in her happier dreams, her subconscious somehow always knew they weren't real.

Saige had always done her best with Mirren. She had listened to Mirren, even when she didn't know what to say in return. She promised her they'd always be friends, and she didn't break her word. She'd managed to cheer Mirren up, make her laugh. But even in her dreams, those times didn't last forever. They wafted into dreams where her and Saige screamed at one another. Dreams where they avoided one another. Dreams where they refused to speak to each other.

Then suddenly Saige became Risa, whispering into the night air that she never wanted to see Mirren again. Over and over and over Mirren could hear Risa's cruel words echoing in her mind, never leaving for even an instant. The worst part was Mirren knew she deserved it.

By the time she cracked her eyes open in the morning to the deafening reminder that she was locked up from that life forever, she thought that if she was even given a single moment with them, all she'd say was that she was sorry and she loved them, cared about them.

Even if they didn't care about her.

Somehow, word had leaked.

Saige was with her family, on their way to get dinner one night, when someone tapped at her shoulder. It was Evie, Risa's friend, and someone Saige hadn't talked to in weeks. Evie's eyes were opened wide. "Saige."

"Evie?" It came out more like a tentative question.

"I heard—you—you're leaving." Evie's face was pale. Saige did a double take. "How?" She'd literally told no one but Risa, though she didn't think Risa had actually been listening. Had Risa told her friend? She must have. How could Risa betray her? Not like it was a surprise—but still. Saige bit down on her lip hard.

"I overheard you telling Risa at school." Evie bit her lip. "That you're going to the Holding."

"Evie," Saige began, her eyes darting around for anyone that might be listening in. "Please, please, please, keep that to yourself. I—"

"So it's true?" Fear laced her expression.

Backpedal. "I'm still figuring it out. I mean. I'd like to. But you know. It might be illegal—"

"You shouldn't do this, Saige," Evie interrupted, shaking her head.

Saige didn't have time to deal with this. She turned and fast-walked to catch up with her family. Archer looked at her questioningly, but she only shook her head.

Word spread surprisingly fast for a town this big. She walked the streets paranoid, constantly looking over her shoulder, ignoring all the strange expressions she got. Rumors were definitely spreading—hopefully what the general population didn't know was that the rumors were true.

She had to tell Archer. He was her closest friend now that Mirren was gone and Risa was refusing to talk to her. He already was wary and concerned, following her when he could, often with an arm around her shoulder.

The fact her cautious and levelheaded brother was so worried scared her. And he didn't even know yet that the rumors were true.

She was going to leave, with Risa if she could convince her, and find Mirren. She wasn't sure how yet, only that she was.

"Archer," she said one night after family time, "I need to talk to you."

He avoided her eyes. "I know what you're going to tell me, Saige."

She kept a steady gaze on him, felt her heart thudding, her nerves rocketing. "And?"

His gaze was weary, his voice shaking. "I can't stop you, Saige," he said after a long moment, running a hand through his thick brown hair. "I know better than to try. And though everything in me goes against this and wants to convince you to stay...to warn you of the dangers out there...of the dangers of coming back here after...If I had known your intentions when you started grilling me about Holding regulations, I don't know I would have told you. But I did, and I can't take it back now." Another heavy sigh, and Saige thought she saw glistens of tears in his eyes.

"As much as I hate to say it...this could be something."

She held onto his every word, listening raptly.

"And who am I to stand in your way?" Suddenly he enveloped her in a tight, strong hug, so unnatural for him that she stood stiff for a moment before coming to her senses and squeezing him back. He pulled away, holding her by the shoulders, and looked her in the eye.

"I'm coming with you, Saige," he said.

"What?" she exclaimed, after a moment's pause.

"What are you talking about?"

"I've been thinking about this," he said quietly. "I can't in good conscience support you doing something like this all on your own. But I also know I can't stop you. So I'm coming with you."

"Mom and Dad will freak," Saige said, because that was the first thing that popped in her mind.

"They will," he agreed. "But they'll know we'll together, and that'll help. Saige." He gripped her arm tightly. "Did you think about the prospect that if this goes right, we could get our sister back, too?"

It took a moment for the words to register, and then she was breathing heavily. Instead of responding to his question, she said, "I was going to leave tonight, after everyone goes to bed. Midnight."

He held her gaze for a moment, a warning tone in his voice. "You'll be doing the same thing Mirren did."

"No," Saige said, shaking her head. "I went to the office today and got the travel permissions. We have to leave at night, because otherwise there'll be too much commotion and people will see and it'll be a mess."

He shook his head. "One travel permission won't cut it with two of us."

"I got a group pass," she quickly said. "Up to six people. There's only three of us."

"Three?" he questioned.

"Risa," she said, avoiding his eyes.

"Right," he said. She thought he'd question her hard on that, but he let it go. "We'll still be out past curfew. That's breaking standard."

"There's no other way," Saige said. "You don't have to come." She walked over to the window, looking out at the bustling afternoon, and crossed her arms.

"Saige," he demanded, walking over to her. "What you're implying is a huge change to our—everything, really. This would change everything if it went through. This isn't really what you're about—changing our whole world?"

"If it's what it takes to bring my friend back," she replied spitefully, looking right at him.

She saw him murmur something under his breath. "What'd you say?" she challenged.

He raised his eyes to look at her tiredly, like he was worn out of her. "Sometimes your loyalty blows me away, Saige," he said. "You do remember what this girl did, right?"

It was the biggest compliment she'd ever gotten from her brother.

"I do remember," she said, and took a deep breath. "Too much, sometimes. The things she said to me echo in my head all the time. But the more I thought about it...is my frustration at her really worthy cause to dismiss her forever? We both know we would have gotten over that. How can I—" Her voice broke off. "How can I let one fight separate us forever?"

When she looked back at her brother, he looked like he was swallowing tears, too.

"Midnight, you said?" he asked quietly.

Saige bit her lip to conceal a smile, and at the same time felt her heart thump. Having Archer in on this made it feel so much more real, and it both excited and scared her.

"Midnight."

"I'll be ready," he said.

The alarm she used for school was only programmed for the standard wake-up times, and besides, it would give her away, so she had to somehow keep herself awake until midnight. She was worried the lack of sleep would mess with her, but turns out sneaking out of her community to go rescue her best friend and possibly change her entire world produced a lot of adrenaline that kept her awake.

She lay silently in bed, watching the numbers on the clock turn, going over everything in her mind again and again, all the what-ifs and assumptions this plan rode on.

Sneaking out alone could get her withdrawn— Archer had been absolutely right—but somehow that didn't scare her. What Saige hadn't told Archer was that she had decided already that even if it meant she got withdrawn herself, she would still go and at least try. If she got withdrawn in the process but saved Mirren, it would be worth it.

Midnight arrived, and she rose on shaking legs and silently loaded a bag with the few things she'd need: some snacks she'd stolen from downstairs—just her portions, so she wasn't robbing any of the family—some extra clothes, her water bottle, a notebook. She pulled the drawstring closed and looped it over her shoulders. She was already dressed, had never even got in pajamas at all.

She felt oddly free and yet trapped all at once. Free, because she'd never broken standard before and it felt weird; but trapped, for what she was about to do didn't have great odds of ending well.

She walked over to the window, hearing her heartbeat in her ears, and looked out over the silent, dark streets. She already knew which way to take; she'd mapped it out the past few days as she walked to and from school and other events.

This was it. This was her moment. She closed her eyes, imagined seeing Mirren's face again. Imagined seeing Cassie again. Then she clung to those images and turned around. Archer was waiting in the doorway, a solemn look on his face and his own bag on his shoulder. It startled her, and she gasped a little, and immediately clapped a hand over her mouth. They both stilled, listening for any telltale sign someone had heard.

Nothing.

Saige followed him, closing the door slowly and silently behind her. She had the sudden longing to wake her parents and tell them what was up; but that was impossible—her parents supported her, but they were loyal to their community. If she'd talked it out weeks ago, they probably could have warmed to the idea. But she hadn't, and throwing this on them last minute was out of the question.

Together, she and Archer crept down the stairs. Saige dropped her shoe putting it on, and the thump echoed in the hall. Again, they both stilled, and Saige felt her breathing become rapid, her head dizzy. If she got this panicked not even out of her own house, she would never make it.

Archer dropped her sweater on her as they headed to the back of the house, and she fumbled with it, pulling it over her arms and her fingers trembling as she struggled to zip it up. She stood up on shaky legs and met Archer's eyes.

He nodded and slowly grasped the doorknob, twisted, pulled. No creak, no noise, nothing.

But then—upstairs: footsteps. Someone was up. Saige couldn't catch her breath.

Archer shoved her out the back door; she didn't have to be told twice. She crouched down against the back of the house, behind a row of bushes, while he silently shut the door behind them, and they both stood stone still for what felt like forever.

"Saige?" His voice was hardly a whisper, and she closed her eyes, trying to regain her senses. What was her plan? She had had it all figured out as of this evening. All this still felt surreal, like she was in a weird sort of dream.

She dropped to her knees and crawled, pressed up against the house on one side, being prickled by the leafy bushes lining the landscape on the other. From this angle, they were perfectly hidden, and the darkness of the back-yards helped. They just had to get to the end of the street, and the first step of the plan would be behind them.

Archer gasped behind her, but she couldn't stop to ask if everything was okay. She could only crawl, faster, faster, ignoring the itchy grass brushing her hands and bare knees—why, oh why, had she worn shorts?—and hope Archer was keeping up.

Her head was low, and all she could smell was the damp smell of earth. Dirt was everywhere. Behind her, Archer panted as he crawled after, right at her heels. How close were they? She couldn't see for the darkness around them; couldn't hear hardly anything at all—and that much was good, it meant nobody had discovered them. She looked up best she could as she crawled, straining her eyes for anything ahead, and kept her mind locked on the image of Mirren.

Finally they reached the end of the street; with a

grunt Saige pulled herself to her feet and flattened herself against the side of the last brick townhouse. Archer followed suit, still panting.

"You okay?" she whispered, and he nodded.

"Let's go." She turned and started creeping along the brick wall, toward the neighboring street.

"Where are we going?" he whispered after her.

Saige cringed. She had forgotten to fill him in on the sketchy part of her plan—as if the whole plan as a whole wasn't sketchy to begin with. "Risa's coming."

"Right," he said, confusion filling his tone, soon replaced by dubiousness. "You got Risa to come?"

"Not exactly." The brick wall was chilly to touch, but she clung to it and the darkness it provided. Not that anyone would be out looking for them—if she had played her cards right, nobody would be looking for them until dawn. The only wild card here was that people knew she wanted to leave.

And someone had been awake in their house. Their parents might already know they were gone. She wasn't sure they'd call for help or anything—they wouldn't risk the withdrawal of their two kids unless absolutely necessary, and, now that she thought about it, they likely already suspected Saige's plan—but still, there was no telling for sure. If they did decide to call, in a matter of minutes their plan could be foiled. And if they got caught now, there was no hope. Getting caught now most certainly meant with-drawal.

Saige fought the panic rising within her. She didn't feel like herself. She wasn't a worrier; she was the spontane-ous one, who did things without thinking. She closed her eyes, desperately trying to resuscitate that side of herself.

"Saige," Archer said, his voice concerned.

"It'll be fine," Saige said quickly. "She does want to come. She just doesn't want to admit it."

"How do you plan to do this, Saige?" he asked her, a cautionary tone in his voice. She brushed it off. "I dropped some hints about leaving tonight earlier today. I think she'll be waiting."

"You—Saige, what were you thinking? Who knows who could have overheard!"

"Obviously they didn't, because we've gotten this far." She chewed her lip, ignoring the faulty logic. They had barely been out five minutes. There was plenty of time left for someone to find them. "Okay, we've got to crawl be-hind the bushes again like we just did. Risa's house is the fifth one down. I'll go first so you know." In the dim moonlight she saw the expression on his face and sighed.

"You don't have to come with, you know. I think Risa will be waiting for me. I'll crawl down a few houses, either get her or not, and come right back. It might be a good idea for you to stay back and keep watch, actually."

But he shook his head. "And what will I do if I see something? I wouldn't have a way to warn you. No, I said I'd come with you, and I will."

She was surprised, but tried not to show it. "Okay."

Crouching down, she scanned the narrow path ahead of them. Please, Risa, be waiting. She wasn't dumb enough to knock on Risa's door. She wasn't sure what was even propelling her down the street now, except for a weird feeling she couldn't describe.

She pressed her hands down in the dirt and started to crawl. The air was yet silent, peaceful, the complete opposite of how she felt. This had to work. This had to work. She didn't know what she'd do with herself if she got stopped now, not when they were so close.

But—the thought suddenly occurred to her— would it be so bad to get caught? Withdrawal would mean seeing Mirren again as well.

But she forcefully shook the thought away. No. That wasn't how she was going to do this. It'd be the selfish way out, and if she was going to do this, she was going to do it right.

At Risa's house, her friend was sitting on the back doorstep, and Saige's heart seemed to stop in her chest. She hadn't really expected Risa to be there. The hints she had dropped had been vague at best, and she hadn't thought Risa was really listening. But here she was.

"Risa?" she said, getting to her knees and wiping her hair from her face. In the darkness she couldn't see the expression on Risa's face.

"Saige," Risa said. "I don't know why I'm doing this."

It was all Saige needed to hear. She took Risa's hand in her mud-caked one and tugged. "Don't think. Just come. Archer's here, too. He'll make sure we stay safe." There was a lighthearted tone in her words, but the irony was loud. They were running away from their community to do something never been done before. Archer could pretty much do nothing to control their safety.

She expected Risa to protest, to once again launch into pointing out all the flaws in her plan. But she was oddly calm as Saige pointed out the path and didn't say a word the entire way back to the end of the street.

"What's the plan now?"

Saige looked over at Risa, then back at Archer, and the gravity of the situation sent her head swimming. Not only were they doing this, but she was leading them.

She closed her eyes to focus her mind, and then opened them to look at the two standing in front of her.

She needed confidence. She knew this was the right thing to do. She knew she could do this.

She clenched her fists and took a deep breath, and explained her plan.

She didn't know why she was here.

Risa wished she could blame Saige, but she knew she had come of her own accord. It had been entirely her decision. And she still didn't even know what had made her make the decision, what made her stay up to meet Saige, what had even caused her to understand what Saige meant when she told Risa how "she and Mirren always loved staying up until midnight at sleepovers." She only knew that, as far as she knew, Saige and Mirren had never slept over, so it had to be some sort of clue. Why Saige wanted her to go was still beyond her understanding.

The plan was straightforward enough. Saige had done her research; she had that much going for her. It was a day's walk away. They would walk bordering the forest line about three-quarters of the way. When the forest ended, the Holding should be in sight. Saige hoped that by that time it'd be dark again, since they'd have to travel in plain sight across fields the last bit of the way, and not hidden by foliage.

There were border patrols, but there were very few, and anyway, they had their travel permissions, which would protect them if they were stopped during the day. Now, in the midst of night, it wouldn't do anything for them. Being out past curfew was against standard, papers or no papers.

The night dragged on as they walked in silence to the end of their community limits and found, as Saige had said, the forest, and hesitantly began creeping through its greenery as quiet as they could manage. Though Saige didn't seem too worried anymore. "We're far from the neighborhoods," she said softly. "If they can hear us from this far away, there's no hope to get out at all."

Risa nodded wordlessly and continued walking.

She had never confused herself more than tonight. If she hated Mirren, why was she here?

The answer hovered in her mind, unafraid to settle itself.

Because she didn't truly hate Mirren.

Why had he come?

Archer had thought he'd come for Saige. But each step closer he took, his heart pounded harder. What he thought was impersonal journey taken for his sister had suddenly become real and personal. Because he had realized who else could be at the end of it.

Archer had never denied to himself the fact he'd never really gotten past it when Cassie was withdrawn. He'd been able to put on a good performance to the rest of the world, but he'd never fooled himself. He let himself hold onto the memory, knowing that accepting the reality as it was would crush him. Cassie had been the sweetest thing alive, and he harbored a secret resentment toward the world around him that could take his sister from him so easily—a resentment he'd also learned to keep tucked away.

He supposed he'd always figured Saige would feel the same, but they'd never communicated so until recently.

Finding out Saige did indeed feel the same felt like a

weight being lifted off his shoulders. Despite his anger, he always knew he still wanted to do something good for his world—for the people he knew and loved. For Saige, for his parents. Doing this trip would jeopardize all of that, and yet, instead of feeling frustration or anxiety, he had an eerie sense of peace. Almost like this trip itself would be that something he'd do to change his world for the better.

He didn't want to think that. It sounded too hopeful, too daring, too dangerous. He knew they'd get withdrawn if this went awry. But he also realized that if, if, if it somehow worked, it could be something seriously big.

And that was something he knew Saige hadn't really realized yet, and he loved her for it. He loved that she wasn't doing this for popularity or to be a hero. She was doing it for her friend, and he somehow also saw she was prepared to face withdrawal herself for it. It scared and amazed him at the same time.

They reached the end of the forest path by dusk, and Saige couldn't have been happier at their timing. She leaned against a tree, squinting off into the distance, and made out the slight outline of a wall against the setting sun. Her palms suddenly felt sweaty. "You guys, I see it."

The stars illuminated their path as they crept across the fields. The building slowly grew closer. Saige kept stealing glances around them as they walked. Was it really going to be this easy?

Had anyone discovered they were gone yet? Were their parents worried, scared? How would the world react in the morning when news spread? Would people come out searching for them?

Her throat felt dry, because she suddenly realized she had no idea what would happen. But still she walked, forward, one step at a time, each step a little closer to her best friend. One step at a time. They were going to make it. Day broke, and she realized how tired she was. Her eyelids drooped and her mind grew foggy. "Rest break?" Her words were broken by a yawn, and suddenly her thoughts grew desperate. They couldn't take a rest break—Mirren was so close!

But Risa was already sitting down, relief flooding her features, and so Saige and Archer followed suit, sinking to the ground and leaning their heads on their bags as makeshift pillows. Saige wanted to scream—they couldn't stop now—what if people came looking? It was daytime, after all, and they'd be easy to spot. But Archer looked asleep already, and before long exhaustion overtook her and every anxious thought slipped away as she fell into a numb sleep.

When they woke, it was dark again. Saige sat up wildly, scanning the surroundings in a hurried frenzy, and it took her several minutes to calm down even after she knew no one was there. Risa sat up next to her and looked at her with hollow but wide eyes, like she couldn't believe she was still here. Archer sat up next, and wordlessly took three apples out of his bag and gave them each one. They were silent as they ate.

When they finished, they stood up together and without a word started walking again. As much as she didn't want to admit it, Saige knew the sleep had been good for her. The more she walked, the more her mind sharpened, and the more her mind sharpened, the faster her heart raced because she realized they were here.

They reached the wall right as the sun set, and Saige squinted her eyes up at the large stone structure. She knew from her history classes it had been standing for decades, but it looked as if it could have been built yesterday. There was no weakness to this wall; the large rocks were solid and fixated together perfectly. She walked up to it, pressed her hand against the cold stone, then her forehead, her eyes closed in concentration but her mind another place entirely.

Mirren was on the other side of this wall. They were so close. This couldn't be the end. They couldn't have gotten all the way here for nothing.

Archer cleared his throat behind her. "Saige? Thoughts?"

"Let's...walk around it. There has to be a door somewhere." Even Saige knew the futility of the plan as the words left her mouth. This wall encircled the entire Holding facility. It'd take forever to walk all around it.

"Never mind...I...let me think."

"We'll find a way." This was from Risa, and Saige looked at her, met her eyes. Risa held the gaze. Saige wanted to question her, but resisted. "We could just try," Risa said. "Walking around. We don't have to go far. What if there is a door right nearby and we miss it because we don't want to look? We can at least try. What else can we do? Climb this thing?"

Risa had a point. Saige turned and leaned back against the stone. "Okay, fair enough. Let's split up, though. Archer, you and I will go right. Risa, you go left. We'll meet back here in fifteen minutes?" She wished she could go on her own, but knew Archer would never stand for it.

Risa nodded quickly. "Yeah, sounds good. I'll come find you if I find anything."

"Same for us." Saige looked at Archer, but his face was impassive. She took a breath. "See you in fifteen minutes."

. . . .

Callum felt it creeping within him, out of nowhere, in the middle of the night, a feeling he couldn't explain, a feeling he couldn't pinpoint, but just a feeling something was wrong.

He tossed and turned in his bed, trying to ignore it,

wishing it away. Then he gave up and got up, paced his room. He felt a pull to do something; but he had no idea what. What could be wrong?

He wasn't going to get any answers just sitting here. He left the room, the bang of the metal door echoing off the empty halls as it shut behind him. He walked silently down, not sure where he was going yet.

After a few minutes he found himself going down the way to Mirren's room, and he wasn't sure why. Well, he could at least check in on her. Callum had not had a newcomer he'd been so worried about in a long time.

Typically by now they'd found their groove. The girls Mirren had come with had adjusted fine. He still wasn't sure how on-track their moral compass was, but for now, they weren't causing problems. Mirren, though, had yet to speak more than a few words at once to anyone or show any sign of emotion.

He still didn't know why she was here. She wouldn't tell him, and while he knew the other girls she'd come with would spill, he really didn't want to ask them. He'd rather Mirren tell him herself when she was ready.

The halls were silent. Finally he reached Mirren's door and suddenly hesitated. What was he thinking? He wasn't about to invade her privacy. He turned to go, except something pulled him back, and he stood there, staring at the door for one moment, and then in a surge of he-didn't-know-what he heaved the door open.

She wasn't there.

He felt his heartbeat in his ears. There was really no scenario where this was good.

And suddenly he knew where she was. How he knew he had no idea, but he knew.

He turned and ran down the halls as fast as his legs would let him; he didn't care anymore about being quiet.

He exited the building, spun around, and ran again toward the wall. Toward the watchtower.

"Please don't let me be too late," he whispered frantically.

One rung at a time. Mirren pulled herself up one rung at time. Higher and higher off the ground. Closer and closer to the top. Callum stopped at the bottom of the ladder and watched in despair as she climbed higher and higher on the ladder used for the watchmen.

They had tried several times to get a ladder to the other side. To get out. But the only materials they had to work with were extra wood from trees inside. Which worked fine for the built-in ladder up their side of the wall, which was rocky and tactile. And as far as they knew, the other side was the same. But to build a ladder that tall without having a wall to work off of would take forever, and it would be nearly impossible to get it over the wall.

Add the fact that there was really nowhere for any

of them to go, and the possibility of ladder on the other side had never gone anywhere.

It was a huge wall, which would mean a huge drop.

If someone fell off the top, the odds of surviving were nonexistent.

His breath came in gasps, and he grabbed the first wooden rung and hauled himself up after her.

"Mirren," he called when he got closer, feeling dizzy already. He had no idea how the watchmen did this. Mirren seemed to have no fear as she climbed, but with every step he felt like the ladder was swaying, though that was impossible—it was built into the wall.

She hesitated for a fraction of a second when he called, then climbed one more and stopped, leaning against the wall, breathing heavily. Callum used the opportunity to catch up. "Mirren, please," he rasped. "Come down."

"I'm not worth anything to anybody," she said back at him, her words carrying as much sting as the sharp wind in the air.

"That's not true, Mirren." Each word stung within him. His grip was sweaty. Hold on, hold on. "Mirren, you know that's not true."

"It is true!" she exclaimed through her tears. "I betrayed everyone who did, Callum. How do you think I ended up here?" And she pulled herself up again up the ladder.

No time to process this. He climbed after her. Focus. *Hold on. Hold on.*

"Nobody cares," she said, and then she swung one leg over the top of the wall, then the next, until she was sitting on top of the wall that kept them in.

"Mirren!" he said again; his voice trembled along with his body—don't look down, don't look down. Emotion propelled him up onto the wall, next to her.

"Look at me, Mirren." She was in the worst place in the world. She had betrayed all those she loved. But that didn't mean she was worthless. Nobody here was. It was his hope he thrived on. If they believed that, they'd all be here, sitting on the wall, wanting to jump with Mirren. But look at them all here—they weren't living the life, but they were living. And life, no matter what, was a gift—a gift Callum wasn't about to just let go.

"Name one person who cares about me, Callum," she said through gritted teeth, without looking at him. "*One* person."

And in a burst of passion, he exclaimed, "I care about you, Mirren."

She turned and stared at him then. Her gaze was hollow, her expression weary. She opened her mouth as if to say something, but nothing came out.

"You're not worthless. You never have been. You're not worthless." He breathed it, gripping the edge of the wall with white knuckles.

"Callum," she said, then. "You don't know what I did."

"I don't have to," he whispered back, the wall seeming to sway beneath his grasp.

"Why?" she said, her face pale, but her eyes suddenly full of deep sadness.

"Because..." He swallowed and then met her eyes.

"Because living here, I've seen many people come through who truly are dangerous. And you're not one of them, Mirren. You may have done something awful, but that's not who you are at heart.

"A few years ago I had to work alongside someone who had planned and put into action a violent attack on their community. And Mirren, do you know what? I could tell. He was a terrible, selfish, arrogant person. You're kind, and you never do anything to hurt anybody else. Last week I saw you accidentally knock the tray out of someone's hands at the cafeteria. You started crying because you felt so bad, Mirren! Criminals don't do that. Wicked people don't care about others."

Her gaze was wobbly. He adjusted his grip on the wall, trying to ignore the swaying feeling consuming him again. "You're not a criminal, Mirren."

"You don't know what I did," she said again, this time weaker. He wanted to scream. "What, Mirren? What did you do that was so bad that you think you deserve to die for it?"

Her stone expression cracked. "I betrayed everyone I know," she choked out. "I stabbed my best friend in the back. I rebelled against my community. I destroyed every relationship I had worth having. And it doesn't even matter, because no one back there cares about me anyway. Nobody cared when I got my orange score for the second time. Nobody cared when I was alone and unwanted by my world. And I know nobody's life has changed since I left." She shook violently, stammering over her words.

"Mirren," he started. "Mirren."

"What?" she screamed at him, suddenly coming alive, and his eyes widened in fear as she grew more animated so close to the edge. "What? What are you going to say to change any of that? I'm glad you think so highly of me, but is that really going to change anything about my surroundings? Is that really going to magically change the past? Is that really going to fix anything? No, it's not!" Her voice grew louder and more passionate. "I'm sick of all this. I can't change anything, and it doesn't even matter if I change now because there's nothing to work toward except this awful, horrid place and I don't know about you, but there's absolutely nothing about it that's even somewhat motivating!" Tears streamed down her red face, her eyes burning with agony.

Callum lifted his hand from its death grip on the wall and found her arm, his whole body shaking as his heart pounded louder than he could ever remember.

"Well, then, Mirren," he said, and despite his inner turbulence his voice was oddly calm. "I'm stuck here, too. Then I guess it won't matter if I decide to jump as well."

Like he'd hoped, her eyes widened in terror, panic coating her expression. "Callum, no, that's not what I—"

Callum met her eyes. "You are not worthless, Mirren," he said.

And then he let go.

Nothing.

Saige ran with her hand trailing along the wall and Archer on her heels, watching closely for anything that could be a hidden entryway or something along those lines anyway, but there was nothing. When they turned to head back to find Risa, she found desperation sinking through her bones and clenched her teeth. They had to find a way.

There was simply no other alternative.

But the wall, stretching on in its perfect wholeness, seemed to mock the idea, taunting her for ever daring to think she could get past it.

When they got back to their meeting spot where they'd left, Risa wasn't there. They walked farther down a bit and found her crouched next to a large, uneven, tumbling pile of rocks.

Saige drew nearer, her mind already turning. "What is this?"

"Did a part of it break?" Archer's voice was laced with doubt, but he looked up all the same, as if part of the top of the wall might have crumbled. But even as Saige realized his thought process she knew it was wrong. This wall was perfectly up kept. It wouldn't be crumbling.

When she looked at Risa, her friend seemed to have reached the same conclusion. "I think it's blocking something."

"Like—?"

"Like I don't know!" Risa cried, blinking. "Like if once, a long time ago, someone carved a hole and escaped or something. Or a part of it broke. Or something. And so they just covered it up."

"Wouldn't they have eventually come back and fixed it?" Archer asked, crouching down to look closer.
"Maybe it's new. I'm not saying it is anything!" said Risa grumpily. "I'm just saying it's odd. Help me start moving these." She lifted a rock up and threw it behind her.

Saige and Archer jumped in, moving pieces of rock as fast as their tired arms would let them, but the pile was huge. And the sun was almost set, taking with it their source of light. Saige stopped after a few minutes, leaning against the wall and looked at Risa, still working ferociously. "Is this worth our time?" she said. "For sure?"

"Have any better ideas?" Risa sniped, but then she quickly softened her tone. "Sorry, Saige...I just....we can't just not try. We have to at least try."

Funny, that was what Saige's perspective had been the past few days.

She resumed hauling rocks away. The cold stone was jagged and sharp against her skin, but she refused to let anything stop her. On they worked, anxiety and adrenaline driving them forward.

"Wait."

The pile diminished to just a few rocks and the only light the dim moonlight, Saige stepped over the rocks now crowding their surroundings and crouched next to the wall. She pressed her fingers against it, and her fingers identified a substance that was definitely not rock. Feeling carefully, she found the edge where it met the rock, and then traced the outline: a circle.

Her breath caught as she continued feeling. A large crack ran the entire length of the strange substance, and she dug her fingernails into it and pulled. Small pieces crumbled away: clay. Hard, dry clay, packed in tightly and now slowly crumbling.

A hole. There had once been a hole through the wall.

"There was a hole here, Risa," she breathed once she found her voice. "They've stopped it up with clay—"

"—and blocked it with this pile." Risa looked pale in the moonlight, not even questioning Saige's discovery. "Can you—I mean—will it come undone?"

"I think so." Saige scraped her fingernails against the clay surface, but only small chunks crumbled away. She grunted and tried again, digging her fingernails into the crack again but achieving no more progress.

Suddenly, Archer jumped up. "Move out of the way."

"What?" "Just do it!"

Saige scrambled away, and watched as Archer lifted a particularly sharp rock and rammed it into the clay, sending pieces of the dry substance flying everywhere and deepening her small indentation. Saige gawked at him, but his grim expression told her he wasn't interested in compliments. He grabbed the rock and heaved it again, and again, clay flew in all directions. He wiped his brow, breathing heavily. "Okay. That should help." He sat down on the rocks and dropped his head into his hands.

Saige and Risa didn't waste any time, pulling and digging at the clay filling until there was a hole golf-ball sized, and then baseball sized. Dry clay stuck beneath Saige's fingernails as she clawed, but she didn't stop until at last they had scraped away every last crumb and there before them was a gap leading into the darkness of the other side.

Saige sat back and once again fought desperation.

"I'll never fit," she cried, fighting sudden tears. The

crevice was hardly big enough for a child. "It won't work."

She tried to wipe her eyes, but the clay dust irritated them. She had forgotten how dirty her hands were. Tears slid down her cheeks, though whether they were from the dirt irritating her eyes or her own emotion she wasn't sure.

"I'll fit."

Risa.

"I'm a lot shorter than you, Saige. I'll fit."

Saige looked at her.

"I have not come all this way to go back," Risa said. "A slightly too small hole is not going to stop me." And she shoved past Saige and crouched down in front of the gap.

"Wait," Saige tried to say, but nothing came out. She swallowed again, her mouth dry, and instead, she said, "You can do this?"

"Excuse me?"

"Like—I thought—you and—"

The hurt registered on Risa's face as she realized what Saige meant, and Saige wished she could take her words back. "Risa, I'm sorry, I just..."

"I have to do this," Risa said, almost more to herself, staring down at the hole.

"What if you don't come back?" babbled Saige, grasping at straws. She wanted to find Mirren. She wanted to be the heroine.

"Saige." Archer, his voice gravelly, as if he knew exactly what she was thinking. "Let her go. She's right. She'll fit better than you or I will."

Saige wanted to cry. Why should she care how they saved Mirren as long as they did? She swallowed a sob. "Go, Risa."

Risa held her gaze for a long moment. "Thank you, Saige."

Then she squeezed her way through the crevice easily and was gone.

Numbness consumed her. Mirren couldn't find feeling in any of her limbs.

But she had to move. She had to climb. Down. Climb down.

She couldn't get the image of Callum falling, down, down, down, out of her head.

Couldn't get his words out of her head, either. Move, move, move.

Be okay, Callum.

Callum—who had possibly just died for her. Why? Her. Mirren. The betrayer. The withdrawee. The Orange student. *Her.*

As soon as she reached the ground, she became aware of loud, angry voices. One of the outside officials, ran at her, and she blinked, stunned. Where had he come from? There had been officials here early that day, but they had all left a long time ago.

"I knew it!" the official crowed, as if he were happy about her friend lying on the ground, motionless. Mirren defensively crouched down next to him, but her fear fixated her eyes on the officials—there were suddenly more of them, sprouting from what seemed like every direction; her heart raced as he approached her. "Backup! Backup!" he screamed into a walkie-talkie device. "I knew if I secretly stayed the night I'd catch you in some criminal act. What'd you do to him, girl?"

Mirren stared at him, then found her words, not even bothering to answer him. "He—fell—you have to help—" What was she thinking? This official who hated her and Callum and everyone here wasn't about to help. So she did the only thing she could think of—she stood up and screamed.

Within moments lights were clicking on and she screamed again. She needed help. Now. Why couldn't they come sooner? The officials were surrounding her, staring at her like she was crazy. They could think that all they wanted. She didn't care what they thought of her. She screamed again. She knew nothing about anything medical.

It was so rare in the world she had come from that really no one did. But there had to be someone here who knew something.

People began flooding out of the buildings, running for her, then noticing the guards and pulling back. She felt hopeless consume her, and she searched for words to say that would help Callum. "Please, help me!"

At the front was one of the guards and one of Callum's friends, Breckan, who had always been kind to Mirren. "You have to help!" she screamed, looking right at him.

Eyeing the guards warily, Breckan boldly walked up to her and crouched down, trying to hold his features together. "Mirren, what happened?"

"Do you know how to help?" Suddenly she was sobbing.

"You need to tell me what happened." He began examining Callum, who still hadn't moved. "Why were you on the wall, Mirren?"

Mirren's vision failed her. She collapsed to the ground, her face buried in her knees, unable to even look. Sobs wracked her fragile frame.

He would know this would get me off the wall.

Callum had tried with his words. He'd risked his life climbing up after her, and she hadn't listened. She'd blocked herself off to his words, his attempts to save her life. He could have just given up and gone back down—he was terrified of the height, she had seen that. But he didn't. Leaving her had never been an option for him.

So he had done what he knew would definitely get off the wall. He knew there was no way she would jump not knowing if he was alive.

The full implication of his actions sank into her bones and shook her from the inside out. He had been willing to die, if it meant saving her.

"You're not worthless, Mirren. You never have been."

And suddenly his words, echoing in her ears, were replaced by other words.

Saige.

"Mirren, your score doesn't define you. It never will define you. You can not let this take you down. You have to show the world! You aren't a worthless part of society. You aren't!"

Risa.

Mirren, what on earth are you talking about? Listen, I don't know what happened, but you're stronger than this.

Ashlyn, and the way she grinned whenever she saw Mirren.

Emory, and the way she checked in on Mirren and always made her laugh. The way she included her sister.

Dawson, and his sarcasm, his funny comments, and his sincere compliments.

Her mother. Her father. Risa. Saige. Emory. Ashlyn. Dawson. They might have their flaws, but they all cared for her in their own way.

The way her mother screamed, her agony drowning out everything else, the day Mirren was arrested.

The hollow look in Emory's eyes, the day she received her Orange score. The fear on Ashlyn's face, the day of her re-test.

You're not worthless, Mirren.

Saige, sitting with her, trying desperately to get Mirren to see what she never could: that she wasn't hopeless, that she wasn't worthless.

Mirren, you might not be a Purple student to the world...but you'll always be a Purple friend to me. You're smart, and kind, loving, caring...and isn't that what really matters?

She had thought her family was avoiding her because they were ashamed of her.

The thought had never crossed her mind that losing her was so hard they couldn't face the reality. That they would be so distraught they wouldn't know how to act.

You're not worthless, Mirren.

Something inside of her twisted as sudden emotion surged through every fiber of her being and she couldn't catch her breath through the agony building within her with each passing moment as the picture before her grew clearer and clearer.

The picture of her world not how she had viewed it—as some place she didn't belong—but how it really was:

a place full her friends and family, not aloof, uncaring creatures, but people who loved her so much that the agony of losing her was too much to bear.

A place she had willingly discarded based on a lie. And the picture that it had taken someone she cared about dying for her to truly see it.

She had thought herself a criminal. She had let her Orange score define her. But if she truly were a criminal, she wouldn't be crouching next to Callum right now.

He had been right.

All along, they had all been right.

And suddenly all she wanted was to see Risa.

To see Saige. Emory. Ashlyn. Dawson.All of them.

Her heart twisted in longing as she sobbed. And Callum's words from the past few months turned themselves over and over in her brain. Callum had lost everything, too. And he hadn't stopped trying. He hadn't given up hope. He hadn't given up at all. He hadn't given up on hope, he hadn't given up on life, and he hadn't given up on her.

She might be helpless, but it was her choice whether or not be hopeless.

You're not worthless, Mirren.

"I don't want to be hopeless anymore," she sobbed into the ground.

And when she lifted her head, she saw Risa.

Risa's foot hit the gravel on the other side, and with a deep breath she pulled herself through.

Darkness descended upon her, and she squinted, but she could only make out faint silhouettes of buildings. Great. If things couldn't be any harder. She took a hesitant step, then a second one, at first hearing nothing but the crunch of gravel under her feet, but slowly she became aware of loud noises, angry voices, coming from what sounded like far off.

This place was huge. She looked over her shoulder, but already she couldn't see the crevice she'd crawled through. The sun had officially set and darkness enveloped her on all sides. Did no one think that the people inside of here might need light? Suddenly she froze, remembering where exactly she was, and panic covered her—who did she think she was, coming in here like some sort of heroine?

She didn't have the slightest idea where to find Mirren, and finding her friend somehow scared her just as much.

Her feet twitched, as if wanting to turn and run back through the crevice, find a way for Saige to do this instead. But she held her ground, keeping her mind focused as she walked, one step at a time. The commotion grew louder and as she walked she saw a lighted area up ahead, illuminated by flickering lampposts. By the dim light she could see a group of people gathered, and she could hear their panicked voices intermingled with commanding orders, and she froze in place again, a terrible feeling working its way up her spine. Fear petrified her, for suddenly she had a sense like one she'd never had before. She knew who was somewhere among that group of people.

She knew like she'd never known anything else before.

Closer she stepped, fear pulsating through her and determination pushing her forward.

Men in uniforms pointed thrusting, commanding fingers at buildings, obviously giving directions for those out to go back in, but nobody was listening. Everyone was talking over each other, many were shouting, and someone was screaming. Except for the men in uniforms, everyone wore the same drab clothing, gray and shapeless, and their faces were dirty, their hair matted. But Risa didn't see that.

She only saw the motionless, silent girl crouched on

the ground in the middle of the frantic crowd, her blonde hair grungy and dirty as it tumbled over her face.

Risa felt like her heart stopped. She had no breath. She was immovable, her feet fastened to the ground, her eyes locked on the girl she'd been told it was for the best she'd never see again.

Her world tilted and spun as promises and reality clashed in her mind. Promises that she'd be fine before long. That this was normal. That this was for the best. That she'd get over this one day and understand that this was the best for everyone involved. Because her best friend had become dangerous.

The only dangerous people here now were the uniformed men, shouting threats to people who, as far as Risa could see, had done nothing wrong tonight.

Was this how it was all the time? The officials constantly reminding the people here what a worthless people they were? What would that feel like—to just walk around and have people scream threats at you?

Was this what Mirren had lived in for the past two months?

The blonde girl shaking on the ground was not who was dangerous.

Risa couldn't breathe.

She'd been told she'd never see Mirren again. But here Mirren was.

If they could be wrong about this, what else could they be wrong about?

Risa swallowed, her throat thick, her eyes still locked on her friend.

Look up, Mirren. Look at me. Prove it's really you.

Mirren—cheerful, encouraging, sweet Mirren.

Prove you're not who they say you are.

I don't believe you are who they say you are. I'm sorry. For what I said.

The words got stuck in her throat.

I don't hate you.

Mirren lifted her head and her bloodshot eyes settled on Risa, and she stared for a long, disbelieving moment.

Risa couldn't take her eyes off her friend. Her hair was grungy and disheveled, and dirt was smudged on her face, but her eyes were alive and burning with emotion.

There was so much ground left between them, but Risa had never felt closer.

Mirren stood up on shaky legs and mouthed Risa's name.

"Hey!" Someone had noticed Risa, and panic shot through her, but she still couldn't move.

"Risa," Mirren mouthed again, and although there had been no sound, Risa heard it clear as day.

Before she even realized what she was doing, she was running to her friend and wrapping her in her arms. Mirren let out a cry and threw her arms around Risa, and they held each other so tightly.

Ever since Saige had left, Linley had turned over their conversation in her mind a thousand times over. Wondering if she had been right in her decision to encourage Saige.

It had been a whole day now. How did she know Saige and Risa were even still alive?

And what would be their fate when they returned?

Some were saying they'd all get withdrawn. Some were petitioning that they all be restored their citizen statuses. Some were hoping they'd fail, arguing that they were setting awful examples. But others were hoping for their success. Linley could see in their faces. Faces of families who'd lost daughters, sons, sisters, brothers. Friends who'd lost friends. Hope for something that had formerly been impossible was surfacing. If Mirren came back and was allowed to stay, it changed everything.

The following day, it was everywhere in the news. It was everywhere: something huge had happened in the Holding, and Linley froze up when she heard. The Holding

274

had been Saige's destination. How did she know this wasn't Saige's doing?

"A withdrawee," the people on the streets were saying, "tried to jump off the wall, and another one saved her life." He had almost died in the process. Some people were saying he had died. Others said he was severely injured. No one knew the truth. The only reason any of them knew anything was because there had been an annual check done that day, and some of the officials had decided to secretly stay the night. They had expected to see terror and wickedness running wild and instead they had found someone willing to sacrifice themselves for their friend.

Linley felt chills when she heard the story, and suddenly she had a strange sensation, remembering Saige's reasons for going: that maybe Mirren still had good within her.

Linley had a brother. A brother who'd been withdrawn in third level for not scoring high enough.

Callum.

Did he not deserve a second chance?

Maybe not everyone inside those walls had good within them—but maybe some of them did. After all, she never had once thought Callum wicked. But Callum hadn't been withdrawn for a treasonous act; he had simply scored too low. Why did his failure equate criminality? Was his low score so awful that it deemed him a life of punishment?

And Mirren—she had committed a treasonous act, but she hadn't done anything directly dangerous to their community. Did that really warrant a lifetime of punishment alongside those who had rebelled in a truly threatening way?

And if Saige was willing to let it go—and Mirren was willing to change—why shouldn't they be allowed to come back?

Such thoughts scared Linley—she'd never dared think so openly before—but nothing like this had ever happened before.

"Why are you here?" Mirren whispered, once she found her breath, still holding onto Risa, her arms shaking but her grip firm.

"I would ask the same." Risa jerked away from Mirren at the voice, trembling, but Mirren shook her head.

"Breckan—I know her."

Risa's eyes found the tired-looking teenager, bags under his eyes, his hair as dirty as Mirren's, saw the fierceness in his eyes but also the exhaustion hiding underneath.

"Mirren," she said, finally finding her voice, and Mirren turned to look at her, and suddenly the reality of the whole situation crashed down upon her again and she lost her words again, her face twisted as tears rolled down that she wasn't sure were from joy or pain.

"Saige is here, Mirren, you have to come—" Words spilled out, but Mirren cut her off. "Saige?" Disbelief filled her eyes, her expression twisted.

"And Archer—Mirren, we really have to go—"

Breckan was looking at her even more oddly now—someone was screaming that there was someone from outside here, though it sounded so distant—panic again, coursing through her veins—

"Please, Mirren, now!" Before it's too late. Before someone stops us.

"Hey, you! You're not in standard Holding clothing!"

"Mirren," Breckan said, grabbing her shoulders and pulling her to face him, and she returned his fiery gaze though she still shook. "Listen to me, because we don't have much time. You obviously know this girl. She's obviously from outside. If she wants to take you—go. Go, Mirren! I'll—Callum—you know what he'd say to do." His face twisted an instant, but then the grim determination returned. "This could be huge, Mirren." He stumbled over his words, his expression fierce. "I'll stall them. You go!"

"Can I really just go?" Mirren whispered. "Aren't we all going to get in trouble again when we get back? This can't be allowed."

Breckan groaned and turned away, but Risa already

had words. "Mirren, we don't know. We just have to try."

Mirren met her eyes, then swallowed and looked back at Breckan.

"I promise I won't forget you," sobbed Mirren. "Any of you."

"I know you won't," he said urgently. "Please, for all of us, go! If they catch you neither of you will ever see light of day again. They won't let Mirren leave, and they won't let you leave, either, now that you've been inside."

He referred to Risa briefly, but then his gaze darted back to Mirren, his voice full of anguish. "Go, Mirren!"

Risa didn't need any further urging. With her hand locked in an iron grip on Mirren's arm, she turned and ran like she'd never run before. With each step, she felt reality fading away. Her heartbeat pounded in her ears, her breaths were ragged, and panic squeezed her chest; she focused only on each step, on making sure she had a hold on Mirren, and before long the hole in the wall came into view.

"Right—there—" she gasped, and when she risked a look back at her friend, Mirren nodded through her tears.

Two more steps, and then they slipped back through the opening and into Mirren's freedom.

"Why are you here?"

Mirren was sobbing again, having found Saige and was clinging to her.

"We're bringing you home, Mirren," Saige rasped, holding onto Mirren.

Home. Not home, as in her cell. Home, as in her family. Her mother, her father. Dawson. Emory. Ashlyn.

People she'd been told she'd never see again.

She shook. This couldn't be real.

She had thought this was the end of the line. That she was done for. That no one cared. But here her friends were, having come all this way for her, having risked everything for her, having done everything—for her.

"Really, Mirren," Saige said, her eyes puffy but her smile huge. "Really!"

"I know," sobbed Mirren. "I can't believe...you're here...that you did this—"

Saige squeezed her friend harder. "You are worth it, Mirren Chase," she whispered. "You have always been worth it."

They didn't have time to waste. Inside, there was still enough going on that nobody had come after them—yet. But Archer was anxious, watching their reunion, his eyes darting back to the gap in the wall. "You guys, we have to move or everything will be for nothing." His voice was hesitant, but his expression firm. Saige hated that her brother was right.

Archer waited impatiently. "Saige—"

Saige looked once again at the girl who was here, really here.

And thought about what could happen if they didn't get out of here.

She grabbed Mirren's hand, and her friend squeezed back. Risa stepped forward, hesitantly, and after a minute, Mirren reached out and grabbed her hand too.

And together, they turned and ran.

Acknowledgements

There are so many people that have been so crucial in the publication of this book, and I am so incredibly grateful to each and every one of you for the time you took to invest in me and my wild writing dreams.

Mom and Dad, as always, thank you for supporting me and always encouraging me and for the time you take to pour into my novels, whether that be in the form of editing, proofreading, formatting help, or cover design. You truly do so much for me and my novels, and I am so beyond grateful. I truly wouldn't have gotten this far without you, so thank you. I love you!

To my brothers: Stevo, greatest thanks for spoiling my book for yourself just so you could help me come up with the title. (Which you did, so thank you!) Also, thanks for always being so involved with my writing. You're awesome. And Jer and Soy, thanks for always unknowingly holding me accountable by constantly asking when my book is coming out. I love you guys!

Marissa, I honestly don't even know where to begin in thanking you. This book truly wouldn't be here without your help, and I am so incredibly grateful for all you did to help *Proof of Purple* become all it could be. From helping me edit, working me through hard scenes, and giving me honest feedback, to listening to me rant and dreaming big with me, you were someone that not only poured into this novel, but also someone who was always there when I needed to be reminded that I could do this. You are amazing and awesome and a true gift from God, so thank you for being you!

A huge shout out goes to all my amazing beta readers—Avery, Sacha, Rebekah, McKenna, Evie, Katelyn, Riley, and Millie, thank you so much for being willing to read this book, even in its ugly early stages, and for taking the time to offer your thoughts, for they were truly invaluable in editing.

To the person who took the most amazing cover photo ever—Evie, thank you so much. And Avery, your lettering made the cover come alive. Thank you!

More thank you's go out to my writerly friends—Katelyn Coker, Riley Rawls, Rebecca Dominick, Millie Florence, and many, many others. Having such amazing and talented writer friends has been such a blessing in my writing journey and I am so grateful for the opportunity to know each one of you!

And finally, to the God who made all of this possible. I would not be here without Him, and this book certainly wouldn't be, for He is the one who has given me this talent and I give Him all the credit. Take this book, Lord. It's yours.

About the Author

J.C. Buchanan is an 18-year-old homeschooler, Christ follower, avid reader, and, of course, a writer. She has been writing since she was four. Her first book, *The Hidden Amethyst*, released when she was 12, followed by *You'll Be Like Faye* when she was 14. She has also published a short novella sequel, *Far Away Faye* (2016). *Proof of Purple* is her third full-length novel.

When she's not writing, thinking about writing, or planning for writing, you can likely find her hanging out at church with all her favorite kids or on some wild adventure (likely to the bookstore) with all her awesome friends. She enjoys bullet journaling, throwing parties, reading, talking about books, reorganizing her bookshelf, thrifting, rearranging her room every six months, taking pictures, and babysitting.

You can find more about her online at **jcbuchanan.com** or you can connect with her on social media!

Instagram: @j.c.buchanan
Pinterest: /jcbuchananbooks
Goodreads: J.C. Buchanan
Facebook: /jcbuchananbooks